The Last Paladin

TOR BOOKS BY KATHLEEN BRYAN

The Serpent and the Rose

The Golden Rose

The Last Paladin

The Last Paladin

KATHLEEN BRYAN

A Tom Doherty Associates Book
New York

THE LAST PALADIN

Map by David Cain

A Tor Book
Published by Tom Doherty Associates, LLC
175 Fifth Avenue
New York, NY 10010

www.tor-forge.com

Tor® is a registered trademark of Tom Doherty Associates, LLC.

ISBN-13: 978-0-7653-1330-0
ISBN-10: 0-7653-1330-8

First Edition: March 2009

Printed in the United States of America

0 9 8 7 6 5 4 3 2 1

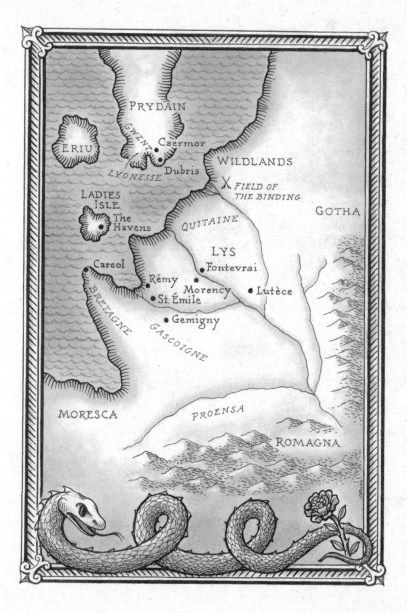

The Last Paladin

1

THE KING WAS dead.

The sea had swallowed him and all his magic, and every traitorous thought and plan that he had cherished. His kingdom was free.

The young queen came over the sea on the wings of a storm, sailing into sunlight and bitter, bone-cracking cold. A tide of wild magic carried her; hosts of wildfolk flew and sailed and swam over and around and beneath the ship that bore her. The air was full of wings and talons and shrill eerie voices, and far and subtle beneath, the slide of scales.

They left her with her escort on a barren and stony shore, streaming ahead of her as if to show her the way. She stood on the shingle, earthbound and struck to the heart, as the full burden of the kingdom fell upon her.

So much darkness. So much sorrow. So many lives lost, souls taken, hearts and spirits broken. By the good God and all his hallows, who was she to take this on herself?

She drew herself up with all the strength she could muster. Her men had moved on past her, some to take the sense of the land, others to greet the folk of her own country who waited on the shingle.

They were not the Knights of the Rose whom she had thought to see, nor were they from her own duchy of Quitaine. These were warriors but not mages, and their commander was a lady in fine wool and furs. The face within the hood was both familiar and unexpected.

As the ship that had brought her over the sea came about and caught the tide, running back swiftly to Prydain, Averil found herself enveloped in a perfumed embrace. "Mathilde," she said as she extricated herself. "Is there trouble?"

Her old ally from the royal court held her at arm's length, smiling, but the dark eyes were somber. "You were wise to insist on coming fast and quiet, lady," said Mathilde. "Come, we'll bring you where it's safe and out of the cold. Then we'll tell you everything."

Averil glanced at the commander of her guard. Mauritius was fully as somber as Mathilde. So were they all, both those who had waited and those who had come over the sea.

She had been locked within herself since she set sail from Prydain. The king was dead; there was a kingdom to claim, to heal, to make new. All of her mind and thought had focused on what she would do and how she would do it.

Now she opened her eyes and saw what her escort had seen since . . . when?

Not so long, or they would have done their best to prevent her from coming across the sea. She looked inside herself, where all of them were, a shining web of magic that wove itself wherever the warrior mages of the Rose still lived.

They had tried to protect her, to shelter her from fear. When she saw what they saw, she could almost understand why they had done it.

Almost. She nodded sharply. "Best we go," she said.

A horse was waiting for her, with her own Squire of the Rose at its head—she should not think of him so, but it was the only truth either of them knew. Gereint's grey eyes were watchful, measuring each man and committing him to memory; measuring Mathilde, too, with intensity that made Averil shiver.

He should have warned her. But now was not the time or the place to speak of it.

He lifted her easily into the saddle. His touch lingered no more than it must. Even in her anger at him above all, she would have preferred that it linger longer. But he was wiser sometimes than she.

She took up the reins. "Follow," she said.

THE LAND WAS sick.

The others knew of the plague that ran across it, but not of the deeper sickness beneath. That was nothing new for Gereint: his eyes persisted in seeing where the rest of the world was blind. Averil felt it because he felt it; it weighed down her spirit, which in turn weighed down his.

The land was sick, and the king's death had done nothing to heal it. Even the return of the Rose to the kingdom's heart, the presence of the Knights' power in the places where it had been broken and cast down, barely lightened the darkness.

THAT FIRST NIGHT of the queen's return to Lys, her escort camped in what had once been a chapter house of the Rose. Its walls still stood; its roof was charred but mostly intact. Averil's Knights walked the borders and restored the wards, hanging bits of glass and living crystal wherever a window or a door had been.

As the sun set, giving way to stars that glittered like the wards of heaven, they gathered round a fire that was half mortal and half magic. After the frugal supper that all had shared, most of the men had either retreated to stand guard or gone to sleep in sheltered corners.

Averil granted the Knights and the lady no such indulgence. Gereint would not sleep while she did not, and one or two others—the Squire Riquier, the Novice Ademar— hung about until the flash of her glance drew them in.

She let them wait while she studied each one. Some suffered that scrutiny more easily than others. Only Mathilde seemed unperturbed, wrapped warmly in her furs and sipping the last of the spiced wine.

At length Averil said, "Tell me, messires, my lady. When were you intending to inform your queen of the plague upon her kingdom?"

It was Mauritius who answered. "Lady, when you were ready, the knowledge was there for your taking."

That was a rebuke, however gently expressed. Averil was in no mood to flinch from it. "Yes, and I have taken it. Was I taught awry, then? On the Isle I learned that when a sorcerer dies, his sorceries die with him. The undead that he raised, the foul things that he wrought, are all undone. Only work of the orders endures beyond death, set forever in glass. Is that a lie? Or did I misunderstand?"

"It is no lie, lady," Mauritius said.

"Truly? And yet when I woke from my soft and coddled dream, I found my kingdom as sore beset as it was when my uncle was king."

"Perhaps it is not as bad as that," said another of the Knights, the tall and deceptively gentle scholar Alain. "The king left a great broil of confusion behind him, armies without will or command, men stripped of souls and wits but not of breath. It is a great plague, and must be destroyed. But without its guiding force, it cannot grow."

"Do you know that?" she asked. "Are you certain? The king was not the only Serpent mage in the world. A gathering of them, a coven if you will, could wreak havoc with the workings that he left behind."

"So they could," Alain said, "but conspiracies need time. Conspiracies of magic, even more so. Your swift action, as little as we liked it then, will have caught them off guard."

"You hope it has," she said.

"Lady," said Mauritius, "if you believe that you are in danger, the ship is not so far away. We'll call it back; you can return to Prydain. We'll bring you here again when the land is safe to live in."

She fixed him with a hard stare. He met it blandly. He knew her best of any but Gereint; he must know what his words would do to her.

That was a game, and she was in no mood to play it. "We

don't know if I am endangered, do we? All we have is a creeping under the skin and a sense of impending doom."

"We have a little more than that, lady," Mathilde said. "The king's men are everywhere, roving bands that are small and seem aimless, but they are a great nuisance. We rode from Lutèce with the Knights and mages who had promised to meet you when you came to land, but all too soon it was clear that they could only make the way safe for you if they devoted themselves to destroying the king's men. So they stayed behind and worked their magics, and I ran ahead with my escort." She paused. Her breath caught just perceptibly. "It's a grievous thing to find and slay the soul-less ones, lady; they're brothers and husbands and sons, after all, and sometimes one recognizes a face."

Averil could not let herself feel the grief of that. She could not feel anything, not now, but determination to do what she must do. "So: they succeeded? They've cleared the way?"

Mathilde shook her head. She seemed close to tears. "There are so many, lady—and more, it seems, the closer we are to the sea. The last Knight rode away from us this morning, aiming toward St. Dol. We eluded several bands thereafter. Something in this country appears to draw them."

"The sea," said Alain. "Their master lies beneath it. It may be we'll be fortunate, and they'll all march blindly into it."

"Maybe," Mathilde said. She did not sound convinced.

"We need to know," said Averil. "If something is bringing them here, we have to find it, to know what it is and why."

"There is no 'we' in that, lady," Mauritius said with all courtesy. "We will seek and find. You will stay as safe as you may."

Averil opened her mouth to object, but such sense as she had restrained her. An uncrowned queen was the most delicate of creatures. There would be no adventuring for her, no riding out, no scouting the land. Her duty was to reach her royal city alive and intact, and take the crown. Nothing else must interfere.

There was nothing to prevent her from searching in other ways. She lowered her eyes and composed her face and said, "In the morning we will ride, with our scouts ahead of us. I must come to Lutèce, messires, my lady—and the sooner, the better."

"That is our plan, lady," said Mauritius. "Tonight we rest and gather our strength. Tomorrow we brave the roads."

They all bowed to that. He had taken command as was proper; it was his rank and station.

Even as he spoke, Averil felt the prickle of awareness in the web as he reached to his brothers for both knowledge and wisdom. They were so few, spread so thin; the burden on them was so great. But Averil could not afford to be merciful. She had to spend what she had, or lose it all.

AVERIL'S UNEASE MADE Gereint's shoulders tighten. He had strength in plenty to give her, but no one could take the weight from her shoulders. That was what it was to be a queen: the burden was hers to carry, no matter how heavy it might be.

He withdrew from the fire if not from her heart. A small

crowd of wildfolk fluttered beyond the wards; their plaintive chirps and chitters tempted Gereint to break the bindings and let them in. But that would not have been wise.

Gereint slipped outside instead and let them come to him. They flocked over and around him, shrilling their gladness. Their touch was as soft as moths' wings, their voices too high almost to hear.

They felt the sickness in the land, too. It was no worse for them than the agony of magic constrained to rigid order, locked in the harsh planes and angles of glass. They suffered the twofold onslaught because Gereint was there, drawing strength from the earth for them all, and because Averil was part of him and he of her. Averil was their queen even before she was queen of mortal Lys.

Mortal Lys was mortally ill, poisoned by the late king's magic. It clotted the rivers and roiled in the earth. The paths of power were knotted and confused; the wild magic was now so weak it was nearly gone, and now so strong it was a danger to itself and all about it.

Gereint knew well the perils of that. Having given these wildfolk what aid he could, he left them to the currents of heaven and slipped back again through the wards. The walls of air and magic brushed past him like wind and fire, but they never touched or harmed him.

"Did I just see what I thought I saw?"

Gereint started. He had settled, unobtrusively he thought, on the edge of the firelight. But Riquier had seen him.

Riquier was both teacher and friend. Gereint trusted him as completely as he trusted anyone in this world. But there were things he never had quite come round to telling his brothers in the Rose.

This would be one of those things. Riquier squatted on his heels beside Gereint, peering at him in the flickering dimness. "You did, didn't you? You walked through great wards as if they hadn't been there at all."

Gereint could lie. Or he could say, "Not exactly through. More around, and inabout."

"Would I understand if you explained?"

Gereint shrugged uncomfortably. "Can you explain how you breathe?"

"That easy, is it?"

Gereint shrugged again. "It's just something I do. Am I in trouble? Is this forbidden?"

"It might be, if anyone knew it was possible." Riquier shook his head. "Every time I think we've got the measure of your magic, you show us whole worlds we'd never thought of. What else can you do that you haven't happened to mention?"

"I don't know," said Gereint. That was not a lie, either, exactly. "Some things I just do. I don't think about them." And some things were between Gereint and Averil.

He held his breath in dread of what secrets Riquier might pry out of him, but his brother Squire only sighed and said, "Thank the good God you're our ally and not our enemy, or you'd be honestly dangerous."

"I am that," said Gereint: "both honest and dangerous."

Whatever Riquier might have replied, he lost it in the flurry as the queen rose and withdrew to her bed. She might not sleep for the depth of her trouble, but she would lie down at least, and close her eyes. That counted for something.

Gereint's watch was not until nearly dawn. He remained by the fire, alone but for the wildfolk who hovered still, high above the camp and its wards.

AVERIL WATCHED HIM from the shelter of the tent Mathilde had insisted she sleep in, even beneath the most solid remnant of the roof. That lady was deeply and peacefully asleep on the other side of it. Averil should rest; she needed all the strength she could muster. But there was no sleep in her.

Gereint had a keener sense of the land than anyone she knew. Maybe it was because he was a farmer's son: he had grown up with his feet in the earth and his eye on the long round of the year. Yet even she, who had been raised on the Ladies' Isle and known little of Lys until she was brought to it by her father's will, scarcely two years past, could feel the wrongness here.

Her great burden and most unwelcome treasure, the pendant of intricate enamelwork that hung always between her breasts, was warm enough to burn. The prisoner within slept as it had for twice a thousand years, no nearer escape than it had ever been. She should have taken heart from that.

Nothing was as it should have been. She burrowed into the warmth of blankets and tried to shut out the world and its sorrows.

Instead she only succeeded in making them stronger. In the darkness and the sharp scent of new wool, she felt the emptiness of bodies stripped of souls, a strong force of them and all too near.

Mathilde had been certain that the king's men wandered without will or intent, gathering in bands of a dozen at most. There were several times that, counted in shivers on her skin, and they did not feel aimless. They felt as if they had a purpose.

Mathilde had not lied, surely; she simply did not know. The soulless were warded against the more common sorts of magic.

Someone had to be leading them. They could not think or act of their own accord; they existed to serve a sorcerer's will. Who that sorcerer was, or what he intended, Averil could not tell. The wards were too strong.

Averil had been a fool to hope that if she came to Lys soon enough, others would not have moved before her. They were all moving at once, and the prize was more than a crown. It was the world.

2

WHEN DAWN TOUCHED the horizon, Averil was still awake, staring at the figure that sat by the ashes of the fire. Except, now, there were two of them: big, broad-shouldered, fair-haired men sitting side by side while the light grew slowly around them.

She had not closed her eyes. She was sure of that. But there he was, shoulder to shoulder with Gereint, conversing softly and amiably in a voice so much like the Squire's that she could not tell them apart. The sight of him made her belly clench.

Peredur was his proper name, though men knew him as Messire Perrin, or as the Myrddin of Gwent in Prydain. He was a mage and an herbalist and a great power of the wild magic. But before he was any of that, he had been a Paladin: the last and youngest of the twelve knights who had walked and worshiped and fought beside the Young God before the Serpent fell.

The rest had died in the natural and mortal way of things, after begetting children who were, some of them,

Averil's ancestors. But Peredur was neither natural nor mortal.

Gereint trusted him with blind and perfect trust. Averil suffered no such delusion. Paladin this creature might have been, but he was born of the wild magic. However much the affairs of mortals might amuse him, they did not matter, not in his heart—if heart he had. He belonged to a different world.

She would gladly have refused to acknowledge his existence. But that was not possible. She set herself in such order as she could and determined to be, at least, polite.

He saw through it, of course. But he indulged her attempt at courtly manners, rose and bowed and greeted her with every appearance of gladness. "Lady! It's a fair morning to be in one's own country."

It was bitter cold, with a threat of snow, but Averil nodded and managed a faint smile. "And you, messire? The queen of Prydain could spare you after all? Or are you returning to your home in the Wildlands?"

His grey eyes were wide and clear and nigh as innocent as Gereint's. "The queen of Lys needs me," he said.

Her brows lifted. "Does she indeed? You'll not be my court mage."

"Of course not, lady," he said. "You have the order of the Rose."

"You think it will not be enough."

"I think," he said with a smile both terrible and sweet, "that the orders will change profoundly before this dance is over. And so, lady, will you."

Averil had already changed more than she had ever wished to. She turned her back on him and went in search of her Knight Commander.

MAURITIUS WAS AWAKE, armed, and breaking his fast. He inclined his head to her and offered a loaf still warm from the baking, split and filled with a wedge of strong cheese from Prydain.

Averil had not known she was hungry until she bit into warm sweet bread and meltingly pungent cheese. It was a moment before she swam up out of bliss to the bitter cold morning and the words she had come to say. "There's an army on the road, messire," she said.

He raised a brow. "Indeed, lady? Have you news? We've cast our nets wide, but apart from a band or two of the king's men, there's nothing to trouble us."

"They're warded against the more familiar magics," she said, "but the land feels them. The wildfolk see them."

Another man might have scoffed, however politely, at her fears, but Mauritius knew her better than that. "How many?" he asked.

"I don't know," she said, and not gladly, either. "Many. More than a hundred. They're not aimless. Someone is leading them. I don't know who, or what, or why. All I can feel is that it, or he, or she, is there."

She had never seen Mauritius either cowed or subdued by any force in earth or heaven, but his face had grown a fraction more haggard. He could not feel what she felt; his magic came from another source, higher and purer maybe, but more vulnerable to the sleights of the Serpent.

He sent out most of his men in twos and threes, riding ahead under strong protections. Only he remained with her, together with Mathilde and her escort: brave men no doubt, but none had so much as a glimmer of magic. Even Peredur rode out alone, to Averil's unabashed relief.

"Seek and scout only," Mauritius instructed the riders. "If the band is small enough, destroy it. But if you meet an army, be wise. Count it, reckon its strength, see who leads it—then come to me."

The brothers of the Rose bowed to his will. Even Gereint offered willing obedience. He was riding with the rest; he could hardly refuse, nor did he want to.

Averil, selfishly, wanted him to stay with her, but he had the clearest sight of any. She needed him to see, so that she could share his eyes.

It was hard to stay behind, to wait for Mathilde's servants to dawdle their way through breaking camp, then to proceed at a proper and ladylike pace while the scouts rode swiftly ahead. She opened the eyes within, and saw as Gereint saw: the long winding road, the leaden sky, the shadow that dimmed the world above and below.

He willed himself to see past it; so therefore did she. Divided perfectly in two, half a Squire of the Rose, half an uncrowned queen, she let her horse carry her toward Lutèce.

GEREINT RODE WITH Ademar as he often had before, searching out the way with all their manifold senses. He was aware of the others dispersed along the roads and tracks and byways, seeking what many reckoned to be a shadow or an illusion.

Gereint knew it was no such thing. There was an army ahead. How far or how many, he could not yet tell. But he would.

The straight way to the royal city ran through a skein of towns and villages interspersed with lordly holdings, manors and castles in which a pair of noble ladies might be expected to take lodging. The first town through which they meant to pass was called Ste.-Alais. In it, Mathilde had assured them, they would find allies and further escort, if Averil would permit it.

Gereint had his doubts of that. For all his efforts, he could not warm to the lady. She had grown up on the Isle as Averil had; she was almost as well bred and perfectly charming. She was certainly pleasing to look at. But she made his skin creep.

He could not explain it. He did his best to hide it—though Averil could not help but know. She marked it for a peasant's suspicion of the wellborn, and no more.

He hoped that was all it was. So much was wrong in this country, it had him all out of his reckoning.

He made himself stop maundering and start scouting. On this cold, raw morning with the first spits of snow beginning to fall, there was no one out on the roads, and precious few wild things to be seen, either. Of wildfolk there was no sign.

But there were things moving, slipping through shadows. Ademar seemed not to notice them. Gereint had to stretch his senses, but there was no mistaking the eyes that watched and the bodies that gathered around and ahead of him.

There were bodies but no souls, eyes but no living minds behind them—eyes that served an alien will. Gereint stopped in the road, knowing he should not, but struck mute and mo-

tionless. He had expected it, though not so soon; and yet it
shocked him deeply. It was so very, utterly wrong.

Ademar halted somewhat ahead, turning with lifted
brow. His expression of vague impatience altered swiftly.
Gereint's face must have been a fair sight, from the reflection in the Novice's eyes.

"What is it?" said Ademar, low enough not to carry far
even in that icy stillness.

"King's men," Gereint said. With an effort that made
him grunt, he urged his horse back into motion. "They're
everywhere, but mostly in front of us."

Ademar frowned. "I can't—"

Gereint leaned toward him, gripping his shoulder, willing sight into him.

His eyes opened wide. His breath hissed between his
teeth. "God's bones! She was right."

"You doubted her?"

Ademar shrugged uncomfortably. "I didn't want it to be
true."

"Neither does she." Gereint's horse jibbed and struck the
earth with a hoof. The gelding could smell what Gereint
could feel: living bodies, but dead within.

He slid from the saddle and tossed the reins to Ademar.
"Wait here. If I don't come back, don't try to find me. Go
and tell Mauritius."

Ademar opened his mouth, probably to protest, but
Gereint did not stay to hear it. Of course the Novice tried
to follow, but Gereint was ready for that. The binding
would not hold him long, but when he did work free of it,
Gereint would be long gone.

He aimed for a steady pace rather than a fast one. He made no attempt at stealth: the land here was open moor and tumbled hillside, and the snow showed every track. Rather, he made himself inconsequential, no more to be noticed than the wind that drifted the snow.

The cold gripped his bones. He let it become a part of him. He was the wind and the snow; he blew across the frozen land, over low rolling hills and fallow fields and bands of woodland.

A village huddled on the wood's edge, straddling the road. There should have been light there and warmth, and mortal noise.

There was movement, and warmth of bodies, but no sound. Dark figures wandered in silence. Some were feeding—not caring what they fed on, whether human or livestock. Others seemed caught in random patterns, motion for its own sake, with no mind or will to guide it.

No commander; no sorcerer. The soulless had gathered here, that was all, drawn to one another by some force that the living could not understand.

Gereint did not want to remember what Mathilde had said: how these had been men once, with names and lives and kin. There was nothing left in these grey faces, these vacant eyes. They were dead, although they walked. They were empty.

He nearly fell into the trap. A flock of wildfolk saved him, flitting above the town just as he began to drop his guard. Their dance was a wild, headlong thing like the swirl of sparks in a gust of wind.

All of those aimless shamblers turned as one. Their movement had not been random at all. Each one might be mindless, but something guided the whole, transforming them into one single, focused weapon.

The wildfolk scattered, not a moment too soon. The bolt of magic that would have blasted them from the sky, dissipated into the strengthening storm. What had begun as snow fell in hissing rain. Where it struck earth, the ground bubbled and steamed.

Gereint recoiled. All his edges burned and stung. But his wits were not entirely gone. He sought the heart of the magic, the mind that wielded those emptied bodies.

That too was a trap, subtler and more deadly than the last. But this time he was prepared for it. He slipped in and around and through, and then out into the clean air.

He shuddered on his knees in a snowdrift, just out of sight of the village. The wildfolk fluttered above him, chittering with rising desperation. He should not stay, he should not tarry, he should go.

So he would, when he could breathe again. His anchor, his Averil—for a hideous instant, she had not existed at all. She was not and could not be and had not ever been.

That was a bleak and baseless lie. He surged to his feet. Almost too late he remembered his glamour. A black blast of sorcery shrieked over him—but he was invisible, inaudible, intangible. He fled in the reek of its wake.

Ademar had broken free of the binding, but he was still waiting at the crossroads. So was Peredur. A scant hour had passed, by the angle of the light, though Gereint would have sworn he had been gone for days.

The Novice greeted him with a mingling of anger and

relief that stung Gereint's raw edges. Peredur was as calm as he always was, the kind of calm that needed two thousand years to grow.

"The king is dead," Gereint said to him, "but the king's sorcerer—I don't think he can die."

"He can," said Peredur, "but it needs more than a colddrake and a mortal ocean."

Gereint could not stop shuddering. "Was he this bad before? Or is this my fault?"

"If this is anyone's fault," said Peredur, "it is his own, for attaching himself like the leech he is to your late and unlamented king. This is the creature raw, naked, and unadorned. He'll find another mask to hide behind."

"Not Averil!" Gereint said fiercely.

"No," said Peredur, "not our lady." Softly though he spoke, the words had the ring of a strong and binding oath.

Gereint turned half-blindly. His horse was there, the reins in his hand. He flung himself into the saddle. Not caring if the others followed, he aimed the horse's head back the way they had come, toward Averil and his heart's home.

3

A VERIL'S ESCORT MADE its slow way eastward, picking its path with maddening caution. The scouts had spread far on all sides; at first it was not obvious, but one by one they faded from perception. A mist had risen on all the roads, concealing magic as well as living presence.

Even earth and wild magic could not penetrate that. Averil was as blind as the rest of them.

Mauritius seemed unperturbed. His power protected all of them as they rode, surrounding them with a crystalline clarity. It was a work of beauty, as effortless as it was potent.

It made Averil's head ache. Her magic had changed; wild magic had entered into it. It was corrupted, a strict mage of the orders would say.

Maybe so. Or maybe it had grown into this newer world. She only wished that it were a little less wild, and had a little less about it of slither and scales.

When Gereint faded into the mist, she swayed in the saddle and nearly fell. Her horse, wise beast, came softly to a halt.

Somewhere amid the fog she was aware that the rest of her escort had halted with her. She stared down at her gloved fingers clenched tightly on the high pommel of the saddle, and tried to stop reaching so desperately for the lost half of herself.

He was alive. She would be dead if he had not been. But she could no longer see through his eyes or feel his heart beating in time with hers.

Voices rose and fell around her. Hooves clattered; the wards parted. Scouts had come back, and the word they brought was as ill as she had feared.

"King's men," they said, "on every road and byway between here and Lutèce. They swarm like ants. Everywhere we search, there is another horde of them."

Averil raised her head. Mauritius was frowning. "What of the other roads? How badly are they beset?"

"Not at all, messire," said those who had followed those roads. "They're as empty as if nothing had ever dreamed of passing there."

That was clear enough. "So," said Mathilde, voicing Averil's thought. "It's not the sea they're seeking. It's the queen."

"So it would seem," Mauritius said. "You tracked the fog within? Did you see where it leads? Or who has wrought it?"

Their denials washed over Averil. Even the Knights could not penetrate the fog.

There was a copse of trees just ahead, a place sheltered from wind and snow. They camped there, set even stronger wards, and built a fire for welcome warmth.

Averil had no appetite for bread or heated wine, but she made herself choke down both. All of the scouts but Gereint and Ademar had returned; every one had the same tale to tell.

She found her wits somewhere and scraped them together. "You know what this must mean," she said. "Have we been betrayed?"

"Perhaps not," Mauritius said. "Our enemies, whoever they might be, would expect the queen to come to Lutèce with all speed and by as straight a road as she may."

"Then she must do no such thing," said Mathilde.

"On the contrary," Averil said. "Now more than ever, we must press on."

"And risk capture or worse?" Mathilde shook her head. "Lady, this plan is doomed to fail."

Averil raised a brow. "You have a better one?"

Before Mathilde could answer, the sentry's call brought them all to the alert. Averil was still half of a useful creature, but she dared indulge in hope.

When she saw the big fair man striding through the trees, her heart nigh leaped from her breast. But it was only Peredur, wearing as somber an expression as he was capable of.

She restrained herself by sheer force of will from leaping up, seizing him, and shaking the truth out of him. Instead, as befit a queen, she remained by the fire and let others accost him.

He wasted no time in idle chatter. "The army is ahead of us," he said as he came near Averil.

Mauritius set her thoughts in words. "The Squire? The Novice?"

"Safe," said Peredur. "They've stayed to watch; the first rank of the enemy have settled in a village not far from here, but if they begin to move, we will know."

"Will we?" Averil asked. "Can you see through the fog?"

"The fog will move, lady," Peredur said perfectly reasonably.

"It's all around us already," said Averil. "We can't delay any longer. We have to ride to Lutèce."

"No, lady," Mathilde said. "If the road ahead is barred, there's no other or safer way to go. Nor do we know yet how large the army is. If all of the king's men have done the same as these, there may be more armies—thousands, even tens of thousands strong."

"We don't know that, either," Averil said. "Speed is our ally. How far are we from the city? Four days? Five?"

"At least six at forced pace, lady," said Mauritius. "Ten or more if we would spare ourselves and the horses, and that is if the storm grows no worse."

"We can't pamper ourselves now. We have to go."

"It's already too late," Mathilde said. "If there are armies gathering and a sorcerer leading them, they'll find and destroy you. You'll never come as far as Lutèce."

"That is true," Peredur said. He had so effaced himself that she had almost dared to hope he had vanished again. But he had been sitting outside the circle, listening in silence. "There is a sorcerer indeed, and a powerful one. Your Squire with the clear sight, lady—he sees the late king's counselor, the false priest; the stink of him lies on this new army. Even as we sit here, it grows, infecting ever more of the land and its people."

"But he is dead," Averil said.

"That is not a human man, lady," said Peredur. "The world was full of his kind once; when the Serpent fell, so did they. But it seems he found a way to live in this altered world, and the power at last, after long years, to make himself lord of it."

"If that is so," said Mauritius, "he'll be looking to take revenge on those who came so near to destroying him."

"Then it's clear what we must do," Mathilde said.

"Yes," said Mauritius. "I've sent word to the Lord Protector in Lutèce. All that we know, he knows. The Knights there and in the lands between will do what must be done."

"Good," said Averil. "They'll make sure my way is clear. We'll break camp now and ride, and pray we stay ahead of the storm."

She did not mean the snow that swirled down through the trees, not entirely. They understood: she saw how their faces closed; how they exchanged glances.

"Lady," Mathilde said after a slight but significant pause. "If it truly is the priest Gamelin behind all of these sorceries, you are in grave peril of your life and soul. Once you as crowned queen take the full power of this realm, you will be the best and indeed the only threat to his dominion. He will stop at nothing to prevent you from reaching either your city or your throne."

"It is Gamelin," said Peredur. "The boy has seen it, and I trust his vision."

"So do I," said Averil. "All the more reason not to delay. You go wherever you please, messire, no matter the time or the distance. Will you take me to Lutèce?"

She had not thought it was possible to catch that most insouciant of mages off guard. Yet he stared at her as if he had never seen her before. Then, as if startled out of all discretion, he laughed.

"Lady," he said, "my powers are no greater than your own. If you must go by those ways, they are yours to venture. But," said Peredur—and indeed, there was always a but—"our enemies will expect no less of you. Not only the world's roads will be guarded against you."

"Even if you bear and conceal me?"

"You are a light in every dark place," said Peredur, "O golden rose."

She wanted to bridle at his mockery, but all laughter had gone from his eyes. She did not want to understand the riddle, either, or to know why he felt the need to speak slant-wise in front of so many loyal allies.

Webs within webs. She chose the simplest way, and spoke it with as little love as she had ever borne him. "You won't help. Then who will?"

"Lady," Mathilde said, "there is a way, if you will: a place where you may be safe, where the enemy will not expect to find you."

"Not Prydain," Averil said, "nor the Isle."

"No," said Mathilde. "I have a manor, lady, not far from here. Nothing distinguishes it from a hundred of its like. It has no great fame; nothing has happened there to mark in memory. And yet, lady, it has been home to my kin and kind since the Young God's day. Its defenses are strong. It may conceal you for as long as necessary, while your servants dispose of the sorcerer and his army."

"No," Averil said. "I do thank you; it's most kind. But I can't lurk and hide and hope he doesn't find me. He will."

"Not while the Rose endures," Mauritius said. "Lady, I believe she is wise as well as generous. This of all enemies will expect you to hasten to Lutèce and your crowning. The straight road is barred. His slaves haunt the lesser roads. He waits for you, lady. But while he fails to find you, his search will buy us time to raise forces against him."

Mathilde nodded. "Exactly. Your Knights no doubt will set traps for him, and lure him far away. Meanwhile, in my manor of Gemigny, you will be safe. It's only for a while, lady. Days, a week, a month at most. Just long enough to clear your path to the throne. It is possible we might even bring the archbishop from Lutèce with the sacred oil and the crown, and invest you there if we must—if we see no other course."

"Indeed," said Mauritius. "No law requires that you be crowned only in Lutèce. It's the rite that matters, that binds you to the realm."

"Better it be Lutèce," Mathilde said before Averil could speak, "but if that cannot be done, we should consider it. We will do all that we can, lady. That we promise you."

Averil's jaw set. They were all so very wise and so very determined to keep her safe. Had she been they, she would have advised the same.

And yet the fog that surrounded them seemed to have crept between Averil and her allies. Even Mauritius was veiled in it. Gereint was lost—who knew if Peredur had told the truth? Who could be certain that her Squire was safe?

If she let herself wander down those paths, she would drive herself mad. That was Serpent magic, creeping in even here, clouding her mind and her wits until she hardly knew what to think.

One thing she was sure of. If she was to be queen, she must refuse to be ordered about. Guided, yes; advised and counseled by those wiser or more skilled in courtcraft than she. But the choices were hers to make.

Even those that, in truth, were not choices at all. She lifted her chin. "Very well," she said. "We will, with thanks, turn aside from the straight path and pause in Gemigny. But only for a while—a day, a handful of days. I must take my crown while there is still a kingdom to rule."

"You will do that, lady," Mathilde said. "By the magic that is in me, I swear it."

Averil shivered in her skin. That was a great oath, and binding. It was meant no doubt to reassure her, but she could only wonder: why so strong a spell for so small a cause? What did Mathilde know that Averil did not?

Maybe the answer was in Gemigny. If so, Averil would discover it. And if not, she would find a way—one way or another.

THE STORM WEAKENED as the day grew older. Gereint was sure by then that the enemy would stay encamped in the gutted village at least until morning—and even if he had judged wrongly, he had no fear of losing the army. He could track it by the emptiness that surrounded it.

That void sucked at his own soul. Ademar looked wan

and ill. For the boy's sake, Gereint left his post and sought the fast-fading memory of light and warmth that was the Rose.

He found them making their slow way southward away from the enemy and the road to Lutèce. As he drew near them, Averil's presence bloomed in him with such power and brilliance that he lost all awareness of the world beyond her.

It was a wonder the whole riding did not stop short at the force of it, but even the Knights seemed oblivious. Maybe Peredur saw, though if he did, he kept silent.

Squire and Novice received no rebuke; they had done as much as they could. Now they all could make as much haste as they might, and hope to reach Gemigny before the enemy grew wise to their plotting.

Gereint took his place beside Averil with a sense of deep relief. Under cover of her mantle, her hand slipped into his. It was thin and cold, and yet strong. Now that he was here, she was ready for anything.

As if in response to her sudden lightness of heart, the snow dwindled and then stopped. The sun ventured out, flying high in an achingly blue sky.

The Knights and the elder Squires rode out again, charged with drawing the enemy's mind and power and lay-ing traps for him along the greater and lesser roads. Mauri-tius kept Riquier with him, and Gereint, and Ademar the Novice. Peredur rode in their place.

Gereint felt his going like the loss of a limb: peculiar, and disconcerting. It was not like the spell that had sundered him from Averil, not quite, but it came from the same place. Everything in this country was twisted out of true.

THEY RODE ON in sunlight, making good speed. Tonight they would camp again beside the road. By midday tomorrow, Mathilde promised, they would be safe in Gemigny.

As the day began to fade into the early winter dusk, the northern horizon turned blue-black, as if night had fallen there in despite of the sun. With no more warning than that, a wall of storm roared upon them.

They fled along the edge of it. There was no shelter, not even a copse of trees: only the bare hills that in summer were clothed in grass.

Gereint knew those hills. Once they had been the edge of his world.

He clutched the high pommel of his saddle, rocked with dizziness even stronger than the buffet of the wind. *Full circle*, he thought.

Two years ago after just such a storm, he had run away from his mother's farm and his own impossible, uncontrollable magic. The only thought he had had then was to beg the Knights to do something, anything, about the thing inside him.

So they had. And now he fled back to his beginning. This road led straight past the farm.

The town of Rémy was not far beyond it in fair weather. But the wind was strengthening; it cut through wool and leather and mail. It pushed them toward the gate and the yard and the all too familiar clutter of outbuildings—

invisible now behind the white wall of snow, but he could feel them, each in its place as it had been since before he could remember.

He on his fine horse in his fine clothes, in the company of knights and a queen, was born to this plain and simple place. It had been in his family for time out of mind: halfway back to the Young God, people said.

There were nobles with less longevity in their pedigrees. But there was nothing noble about his mother's ancestry, and his own was even more lowly. He did not even know who his father was. He was the great anomaly: a Squire of the Rose without birth or lineage.

Somehow he had made his way to the front of the company. No one spoke, even if a mortal voice could have been heard above the shriek of the wind.

There was nothing to be said. Either they took shelter here—whatever they found within—or they died. They had no other choice.

The gate loomed before Gereint, so close he nearly rode into it. As he dismounted, the wind did its best to batter him to his knees. His horse groaned and braced against it.

The gate was barred. That need not be any obstacle to Gereint. But there were courtesies, and he was what he had grown to be.

He raised his fist and hammered on the gate—just as, two years ago, another Squire had done, in another storm. He almost expected to find himself face to face with the raw boy he had been, so full of untutored magic that he was a menace to himself and everyone around him.

That boy was gone, run off with the Knights of the Rose. The woman who opened the gate was older, stronger in her way, and not visibly dismayed to be descended upon by a crowd of gentry.

She regarded her son without recognition: seeing the size of him, the armor, and the shivering horse beside him, and taking no notice of the face inside the hood. He had half hoped for that, but the pain of it surprised him.

What had he expected, after all? Enid would hardly be likely to fall weeping on his neck. That had never been her way. But he would have thought she would at least find him familiar.

She gave him no time to scrape words together. Her eye flicked past him, counted bodies in the snow, widened slightly at the number but betrayed no sign of dismay.

The suspicion in them was hardly new, but the searching depth of her glance spoke of troubles that would have been unthinkable before Gereint left her to manage alone. She was making sure that their souls were in their bodies. That was as clear as if she had set it in words.

"Come in," she said, "quick, before the wind eats you alive."

Gereint bowed and followed her through the gate into the yard that he knew so well. None of it had changed; everything was where it had been, in scrupulous order.

She must have hired help, but if she had, it was not in evidence tonight. No one else came to tend the horses or to settle the men-at-arms in the warmth of the hayloft. The house, when she led the high ones to it, was empty but for her.

Gereint's old cloak still hung on the peg by the door,

with his worn and by now far outgrown boots below it. Everything else was exactly as he remembered it.

The ladies would sleep in her bed in the closet of a room above the hearth. The men had the attic that had been Gereint's. It had always been so when there were guests off the road.

While she showed the ladies to their room and pointed the men toward theirs, Gereint stayed below in the big open kitchen. It was the easiest thing in the world to take off his Squire's mantle and hang it on the peg over his old one, then set to work.

He fetched wood from the shed to build up the fire, and found the cauldron in its cupboard and hung it over the hearth, just as he had always done. When he reached for the bucket to fetch water from the well, Enid's hand was on it first, and her eyes were on him, clear and hard as the glass in which his teachers had taught him to contain a little of his magic.

There was no glass in this place—not even in the windows; not a goblet or a beaker or a bit of sparkle to catch the sun. Magic of that kind could gain no purchase here. His magic . . .

"So," his mother said. "That's where you got to. You couldn't write a letter?"

Gereint flushed from crown to toes. Never mind that he had been running for his life, wandering in exile, and working great and terrible magics. Here he was a fool of a boy who had vanished without a word.

He had no words to say now, and no protest when she cuffed him—not too hard—and then paused. Maybe she had not noticed it before; maybe the fire's flicker caught it so that it flared into sudden light. Her finger brushed the silver rose embroidered over his heart.

Her face wore no expression. Gereint waited, perfectly still, for the blast he was sure was coming. Of all things he could have been or done, this had to be the worst. She hated magic; loathed it, despised it, would have nothing to do with it. She had raised him in utter ignorance of the powers that were in him. And he had become a mage of the greatest order of them all.

She drew her breath in sharply, then let it go. "What did you do? Lie about your father?"

"There's no lying to a Knight," Gereint said.

"They don't take the likes of us," said Enid.

"So I've heard," he said. He reached past her for the wooden bucket.

Her lips were tight. She always looked angry, but there was more to this than simple temper. "I tried to save you," she said.

"From what?" He did not mean to loom over her, but he could not help it. "From myself? I was perilous close to blowing apart when the Rose found me. But for them, I'd be running mad in the Wildlands—or worse."

"Not you," she said. "You're stronger than that."

"No one is that strong," said Gereint. "We'd both have died of my ignorance."

There was a slight but potent pause. Then she said, "You came back."

"Not by my choice."

"You hate me," she said. There was no telling what she

thought of that. Mage or no, he could read her no more easily now than he ever had.

He shook his head. "I probably should. But I don't."

"Then you're a fool."

"I am." He turned away from her, bucket in hand, aiming for the well.

She made no move to stop him. When he came back, shivering and blasted with wind and snow, she had a fat haunch of mutton turning on the spit and a mound of roots and herbs ready for the pot. As he poured the water in, his eyes and nose stung pleasurably with the pungency of onions and garlic.

Their quarrel had ended in silence as always. It was comfort of a sort, a kind of barbed amity. In time, the edges would wear off and the causes of contention be forgotten, and they would rub on together until the next battle.

There would be no more of that. He was not going to stay. All this familiarity had stopped being home a long time ago. He belonged to the Rose now, and to the lady who came down into the firelight and the cooking smells, kilted up her skirts and rolled up her sleeves and set to baking bread while the stew bubbled and the spit turned.

Averil had played the servant before to good effect. She was more at ease in that office, truth be told, than the one her birth and destiny entitled her to.

Gereint could appreciate the irony. He was better suited to be a knight and mage than the farmer's son he was born to be.

Tonight they worked together, and his mother with them, in silence that was remarkably companionable. In time the others came down, except the Lady Mathilde, who professed herself indisposed.

Averil would have tended her, but the Knights would have none of that. Ademar took on the duty, and none too reluctantly, either. He was of an age to be especially captivated by a woman's face.

They ate amply and well; so did the men in the barn, assisted by a barrel of Enid's own brown ale. In the house there was ale, and apples dipped in honey, and cakes with clotted cream and a pot of dearly hoarded berries stewed in honey and a precious bit of spice, the last of the long-gone summer.

Gereint had eaten less well at a queen's table, though it would hardly be wise for him to say so. Mauritius said it instead, with native and instinctive courtesy.

Enid was never one to blush or smile, but Gereint could tell she was pleased. She barely scoffed, and she filled Mauritius' cup again, to the brim: a great gift from a woman as thrifty as she was.

4

WELL AFTER THE last of the men had stumbled up to the loft, Averil stayed by the fire. She had helped Gereint with the washing up; when he wrapped his mantle around him and went to sleep near the hearth, she sat with knees drawn up and chin resting on them, letting the warmth and the fiery visions wash over her.

They were full of dragons tonight, sinuous shapes that were both greater and more magical than mortal serpents: firedrakes, but kin to the great cold-drake that had destroyed the king's fleet. They danced in the flames, heedless of mortal wars, though the outcome of this one might touch them as it touched all else.

And yet, in spite of her many troubles, her desperation, her sense of deathly urgency, Averil was strangely at peace. She felt if she had stepped out of the world—if only for a night.

None of her companions had told Averil who their host was, but even if she had not known from the jangle of confusion and tension that rode in Gereint, it was obvious in everything both Enid and her son did.

It could not be coincidence that they were here. The wind had led them straight to the gate. It was an omen, Averil thought: a glimmer of hope. If Gereint could find his way home, then so could she.

Enid was wakeful, too. She sat in the stiff wooden chair, stitching a smock with fingers that needed neither light nor eyes to see.

She bore little resemblance to Gereint. They shared a certain robustness of frame, and Enid's firm jaw and level brows recalled his, but the rest must come from the father no one spoke of.

Whoever he had been, he had had magic to spare. Enid had none whatever. She was that rarity in this world, a human creature whom the power had altogether passed by.

It did not diminish her in the slightest. She was as strong as the bones of the earth, rooted in it, in perfect surety of what she was and who she was and what she was meant to be.

Averil could learn from her. Tonight, while the wind howled without and the snow fell deep and hard, she studied that potent stillness and sought some image of it in herself.

The fire was fading. Averil laid a new log on the embers of the old. The flames rose anew, bathing her face in blessed heat.

"Tell me something," Enid said. Her voice seemed to grow out of the fire's crackling.

Averil drew back from the fire and turned. Enid fixed her with a penetrating stare. "You're not a servant, are you?"

"No more than your son is," Averil said.

Enid shook her head in quick annoyance. "No games. Not in my house. You all keep secrets—that's fair enough. I don't want to know anything that might harm either you or me. But I see the way you look at the boy. If you break his heart, lady, you'll have me to answer to."

"And if he breaks mine?"

"You'll mend," Enid said. "You may never let a man near you again, but you'll be strong. Women are. When a man breaks, he stays broken."

Averil had her doubts of that, but she was a guest here. She kept them to herself. "Whatever is between us, nothing will come of it. Knights don't marry."

"Is he a Knight yet?"

"No, but he will be."

"Will he?"

"I'm sure of it," Averil said.

"That's never what I raised him to be."

"I wasn't raised to be what I am, either," said Averil.

"It's that kind of world," Enid said. "Be careful, lady. Of him and of yourself."

It was too late for that. Averil shook her head and sighed. "I can't promise you anything but that I'll love him. I might destroy him. If that's what must be, it will be."

"Then I'll come for you," said Enid calmly.

Averil had no doubt that she would. It was reassuring in

its way. If she had had a mother living, she would have wanted such a one—even as fierce and manifestly difficult as Enid was.

THE STORM RAGED for three days. There was no traveling in that; it was enough to struggle across the farmyard through head-high drifts of snow to tend the animals and the men who had turned the hayloft into a guardroom. They ran a rope from the house door to the stable, and that guided them through the world of unrelenting white.

At least, Gereint reflected, if they could not venture the roads, neither could the sorcerer's slaves. Yet he would have been glad to try.

It was not that he was made unwelcome, or that he felt unduly out of place. It was a deeper thing, a kind of misery, because this had been home for so long, and now it was not.

Throughout that time of waiting, the Lady Mathilde kept to her room. Strong wards lay on it; sometimes Gereint felt the hum of magic in his bones.

No one else seemed alarmed by it. He told himself he was being unreasonably suspicious.

So did Mauritius when Gereint scraped together his courage and approached the Knight. "This is her generosity," Mauritius said, "and her care for queen and kingdom. She protects us all here as she means to do in her own manor, guarding us against the enemy. She's left us free to rest and restore our strength."

"I'm sure, messire," Gereint said, "but something doesn't feel right. What if she's not what she pretends? What if—"

"Nothing in this kingdom feels right," said Mauritius, "and you have more to contend with here than the rest of us. Be sure that we're watching, messire; if there's any treachery afoot, we'll do our best not to be caught unawares."

Gereint was doubtful still, but he had no sensible objection to offer—only the itching inside his skin. He bowed and shut his mouth and did his best to be the obedient Squire.

He had more than enough to occupy his mind. The brothers of the Rose were safe wherever they had found shelter. The four who had come to the farm rested as warriors did during a lull in battle, filling the days with lessons and arms practice.

Gereint especially had need of the last. However powerful he was in magic, he was shamefully weak with weapons. He had come to them late, and he had a great deal of learning to do before he came close to the skill of these nobles who had been born to ride and fight.

He was getting better. Even Riquier admitted that, and Riquier had struggled longest and hardest of any of them to turn Gereint into a fighting man.

It was more than odd to be practicing the art here, where he had grown up in ignorance of any such thing. His mother said nothing of it, either good or ill, but it seemed clear enough to him what she thought.

He was a disappointment, with his fine clothes and his lordly airs. He did no credit to his ancestors, honest farmers all, with no taint of the gentry.

No taint of magic, either. He was not asked to practice

that, but the shadow of it was on everything he did. The order of the Rose was an order of mages, and he was strong—how strong, no one knew.

That was not spoken of in this place. There were interesting silences and moments of subtle discomfort. Yet, with nothing to be done but wait, they settled into a kind of peace.

On the morning of the third day, the wind howled as loudly as ever. The snow had risen to the rafters; the path to the barn was a white tunnel. The horses were growing restless, and the men held grimly to patience.

Gereint tended the horses. It had been his allotted task when he was a mere hanger-on. Now that he was a Squire, he saw no reason to stop.

It was peaceful work, surrounded by the warmth of the big beasts' bodies. Sometimes one or more of Mathilde's men would come to lend a hand, but this morning they were occupied elsewhere.

He happened to notice just then that the wind had slackened. It had done that now and then since the storm began, but never for long. In the unwonted silence, he heard the rattle of the door, and voices speaking.

One was new here, but he knew it well. He tossed the last armful of hay into the last manger and made haste down the rows of stalls.

Ademar had let Peredur in. As the Novice heaved the door shut once more, the wind smote with renewed force, so hard the whole barn shook.

Peredur's mantle was dusted with snow, but he did not

look as if he had traveled long leagues through hell's own storm. His fair hair was barely ruffled, and his boots were nearly dry.

Averil would have somewhat to say of that. Gereint caught himself in a craven desire to keep Peredur's presence from her for as long as he might.

That was foolish, of course. She knew because Gereint knew. Soon enough, they all would.

"Is there news, messire?" Gereint asked.

Peredur nodded. It was difficult to tell from his expression whether that news was good or ill. Nor would he tell it until they were all together.

Mauritius and Riquier were in the house with Averil. Gereint led Peredur there: a fair feat, traveling those few yards, though by now he was all too accustomed to it.

It was wonderfully warm within, firelit and lamplit. Mauritius and Riquier kneaded bread on the table near the hearth. Enid and Averil were spinning wool, fair brown head beside bright red-gold in the fire's gleam.

Gereint stepped aside to let Peredur in, with Ademar close behind. Averil's sudden chill he had expected, but not Enid's. His mother's face had gone completely blank.

Even more startling, so had Peredur's. He was often inscrutable, but this was different. It was the same stillness, in every particular, that had possessed Enid.

When she spoke, her voice was as flat as her expression. "I will not have that in my house."

"Mother," Gereint said, "this is—"

"I know that it is," she said. "It has no place here."

"Mother—"

"It's no matter," Peredur said with remarkable gentleness. "I'll say my word and go."

"In this storm?" Gereint did not often lose his temper, but this made him angry out of all reason. Never mind that Peredur had obviously come here by other ways than mortal, and could leave by those same ways. There were laws and courtesies. Not even Enid was exempt from them.

"You will stay," Gereint said. "Promise to work no magic, that's all we'll ask of you."

Gereint braced for the blast of his mother's wrath, but none came. She flung up her hands as if to thrust the lot of them away, snatched her cloak from its peg, and strode toward the door.

Gereint gaped like the idiot he was. Mauritius, nearer the door than he, reached it in a long stride and barred her way. "Madam," he said. His voice was monumentally calm. "Whatever ill will you bear this man or what he is, for the good God's sake, take thought for your safety."

"I'm as safe in my own barn as I'll be here," Enid said. "Let me go, sir."

Mauritius frowned, then shrugged. But as he began to move aside, Peredur said, "No. I'll go. This is her place. I don't belong in it."

"By that token," Gereint said, "none of us does. I'll go, too. We'll all go."

"Don't do that," Peredur said mildly, but the words held the force of a command.

Gereint should study such magic. His own had precious little subtlety, though he was learning, slowly, to rein it in.

Those were strange cold thoughts, but they fit somehow with the confusion of this place and these people. Gereint's anger had faded. "You have news," he said to Peredur.

"Proof, rather," said Peredur, "of what we already knew. The king's sorcerer lives. The army we saw is indeed his— and it is but a fraction of the forces he has arrayed against us."

Mauritius' face betrayed neither shock nor dismay. "Show us," he said.

Without hesitation and without apology, Peredur drew magic out of earth and air, round and gleaming like a glass in his lifted hands. Through the glass they saw a room, a blur of tapestry, a man's long pale face crowned with the tonsure of a priest. Maybe it was the magic, maybe Gereint's own hatred of the man, but it seemed that white skin had a faint sheen of scales.

There were others near him, shadows that would not come clear even for Gereint's sight. He strained to see; it was urgent that he know them. But they flickered and vanished before a new vision: a land overrun, armies massing on every road and hillside, and all of it wrapped in a blinding fog of magic.

A minuscule part of Gereint wondered if Peredur had been one of the shadows that surrounded the sorcerer. But that was absurd. Peredur was, had been, a Paladin. He would never in his long life turn toward the Serpent.

5

W HEN HIS WORKING had melted into air, Peredur said, "Now I'll go."

"Don't."

They all stared at Enid. She was as expressionless as ever. "Stay until the storm passes."

"There is no need—" he began.

"Stay," she said.

Magic or no, she had the same gift of command as Peredur. "You are certain?" he asked her.

"No," she said, "but you'll stay."

He bowed to her with no mockery that Gereint could discern.

Gereint's confusion had shifted its focus. He was not sure he liked what it was changing to, or believed in it, either. It was too improbable.

And yet, was it impossible? The tension between his mother and the Paladin was subtly but profoundly different from Averil's inborn and intractable mistrust.

They knew each other well, from the look of it. How

well, he was afraid to guess. Because if he was right—if they really were what he thought they were, then—

No one was paying attention to Gereint. Even Averil was barely aware of him, caught up in the arrival of Mathilde, who had come down at last from her days-long retreat.

There was another cause for confusion, but it mattered little just now. While the others fussed about, waiting on the lady, Gereint studied his hand.

It was a sturdy hand, like the rest of him, and strong. It was taking slowly to the arts of knightly weapons, but put it to a plow or a mattock and it knew well what to do. Some calluses on it had faded, while others had grown instead: shifting as he had, from farmer's son to Knight of the Rose.

Peredur's hand, quiet at his side as he watched the flurry over the lady's coming, was quite like it in shape and size. It had the same square palm and long fingers, even the same slight crookedness in the smallest finger.

Gereint resisted the urge to thrust both hands behind his back. There was no hiding the rest of him, the likeness anyone could see, if anyone cared about it at all.

He went out. There was the storm, of course, but it was no matter. He simply had to step as he did through wards, around and inabout.

Pity he could not step all the way to Lutèce. But he was not as strong as that.

The barn was the best haven he could think of on such short notice. Up in the loft, the men of Mathilde's escort went not so slowly out of their minds with boredom. Down in the stalls, the horses did much the same.

The mule, into whose stall he slipped, was more philosophical. Time spent warm, dry, and free of work, with a manger full of hay, seemed like time well spent. It slanted a long ear at his sudden presence, but did not begrudge it.

The mule always had found him tolerable. He sat in the corner on the clean dry straw, hugged his knees and tried to become a perfect blank.

No human thing could attain such a state. Even with magic, even in shock, some part of him remained to twitch and babble.

He had never expected to meet his father. He had hoped for it as children do—but there had been so much else to think of, and so much magic to do battle with, that it had dwindled to a shadow and a dream.

He had been certain that his mother, in the only lapse of her life, had slipped into indiscretion with an ordinary mortal. Maybe it was a lord or a priest, or more likely another honest farmer who for whatever good and sufficient reason was not to know he had a son. That it was someone with magic had been a reasonable enough conjecture, but magic was a common thing in this world.

That Gereint truly might be godborn had never occurred to him. Such things did not happen in these days. The gods were gone, fled from the Young God's Church and the orders of magic.

He had reckoned without the lesser powers that had stayed, the half-gods and daimons and the wild mages whose magic had devoured them entire. He had been practical, he thought, as his mother had taught him to be. All his extravagance had focused on dreams of a duchess who had become a queen.

As for what this new knowledge did to those dreams . . .

It was more than he could hold in his mind all at once. It explained so much, and made so much clear—but nothing was simpler.

Better if his father had been a farmer with a wife and a family and a quite natural aversion to scandal. He had not been raised for this.

He had not been raised to be a Knight, either, and yet here he was, with the Rose over his heart. The magic in his blood had driven him to that. Now he knew why.

"Did you know?"

Peredur could hear him wherever either of them was. As it happened, he was standing at the door of the stall, looking in. He might have been there for a moment or an hour; Gereint could not have said. "That she had a child? Not until I saw you."

"The first time?"

"You hold your head like her," said Peredur.

That was odd, but no odder than the one who said it. "I can understand," Gereint said, "how you might have promised to come back, but time passes differently when your world runs in eons instead of days. You forgot, or never knew, how swift those days pass for mortals. I can understand why she might turn against all that was magical, if one like you had loved her and left her. But this I can't properly see. Why Enid? Are there hundreds of others? Thousands? Is the world sown with my brothers and sisters?"

"As far as I know," Peredur said, "there's only you."

Gereint sat back against the wall. "Oh, come now. I may be a yokel, but I'm not a fool."

"That is the truth," said Peredur. "There have been other lovers, yes—a few over the long years. But none ever conceived a child. I reckoned I was like yon mule. Most of us are."

Gereint quelled the uprushing of painful laughter. If he started, he would not be able to stop. He made himself focus on the question he had asked, that Peredur had not yet answered. "Why Enid? Of all women who might have drawn your eye, why did you choose her?"

"Need it have been I who did the choosing?"

Gereint answered with a hard stare.

Peredur spread his hands—not in surrender, not exactly. "Of course you don't see it; you're her child, and she has grown fierce in her maturity. She was splendid when she was young. I met her in the horse market in Sévigny. She had a pair of mares to sell, and some of the traders thought to take advantage of the simple country maid."

"And you came to her rescue," Gereint said.

Peredur burst out laughing. "Oh, no! She tied their poor feeble wits in knots, got a fair price and then some for each of the mares, and left them wondering what had struck them. I was enthralled. She had no magic that any mage would reckon, but there was such power in her as few creatures possess, mortal or otherwise."

Gereint nodded somewhat grudgingly. "She has a fair force of will, my mother does."

"So she does. She cast her eye on me, and seemed to find

me pleasing, though she said the harness I was selling was grossly overpriced, and showed me how to remedy a fault in the stitching. One thing led to another, and one day opened on the next, and before we knew it we'd gone from summer into autumn and a messenger had come: her father was dead, her mother long gone, and there was no one left to take on the farm.

"I urged her to sell it; she could stay with me, I could settle, there were towns enough that could use an herb-healer. But the earth of this place is in her bones."

"You could have come with her. Rémy hasn't had an herb-healer since anyone can remember."

"So she told me," Peredur said. "We were ready to go. Our belongings were packed, the cart was waiting. But that night the old king died. I was—I still am—bound to this kingdom as I am to Prydain, by oaths as old as I and rather stronger. I had to go away, for a day or two I thought, to see the new king crowned."

"Clodovec," said Gereint, choking on the name.

"Clodovec," said Peredur.

"And the day or two became a month, and then a year," Gereint said, "and Clodovec was Clodovec, which caused you more than enough distraction. Then there was Prydain, and the Wildlands, and probably a dozen more countries and oaths and bindings that I know nothing of, and you never quite got round to finding your lover again. She came home alone, turned down every man who offered for her, gave birth to me and raised me and taught me that magic was never for the likes of us. Even when it was obvious that I had more of it than any mortal had a right to."

Gereint was not bitter. It was all truth, what he said. If it caused Peredur pain, then so it did. Enid had lived with pain and shame for much of her life since she came back to Rémy. It was only fair her lover share a little of it.

Her lover. Peredur, last of the Paladins. Gereint could not yet think of him as *father*. It would be a long while before he was able to do that.

Gereint pushed himself to his feet. "I can't think about this now," he said. "This kingdom is drowning in sorcery, the Serpent is closer to waking than it's been since anyone but you can remember, and every one of us needs every scrap of strength."

"This isn't strength?" Peredur asked. "If you know what you are, you can master it."

"Is there time for that? Is there time for anything but a mad run to Lutèce and a prayer we don't get there too late?"

"That time may save us all."

Gereint shook his head hard. "I'm not your Young God, born to make the world anew. If that's anyone's destiny, it's our lady's. I'm barely ready to be a Squire."

"No one is the Young God," said Peredur. "Even he was not, mostly—except when he had to be."

"No," said Gereint. "No, I can't be what he was. Don't try to force it on me. I know what I am and what I'm useful for, and that's what I'll be. I belong to my queen, and I'll defend her with all the power I have. That's all I can hope to do."

Peredur bent his head. "No one can ask for more."

Just then, Gereint understood perfectly how Averil felt about this—man, daimon, whatever he was. His immediate and profound trust had been the blood calling, no more. The son yearned to trust his father; it was bred in him.

But what if he could not trust Peredur? What if this was no ally but the worst of enemies? Who knew what he truly was, or what purposes he followed, or for whom? Who ever had known?

Gereint made no effort to be courteous. He dived back into the Rose, to the life and self he knew best, and the duties and obligations that held his excess of magic so tenuously in check.

6

MATHILDE SEEMED MUCH refreshed after her three days' retreat, and ready to face whatever lay ahead. "The storm will pass soon," she said. "When it does—"

"Will it?" Averil asked. "What if sorcery bred it? It can keep us trapped here forever."

"This is a storm of earth," Mathilde said. "I've searched all the ways of power, and it will leave us in the night."

"How long after that, then, before the roads are open?" Averil did not know why she was so contrary. It seemed as if her tongue spoke of its own will. Of course Mathilde told the truth, and it would be a mercy if they all left before they drained the last of their host's winter stores.

"We can make our way onward tomorrow, if the snow stops," Mauritius said; then, as if he had read her thoughts: "We'll send a caravan of provisions from the nearest market town, as soon as one can safely pass."

"No need."

They had forgotten Enid was there. She stood by the door with her cloak still in her hand and her face as blank as ever. "I don't need to be paid," she said, "and you don't need to go if it's safer for you to stay."

"That is more than generous," Mathilde said, "and we are grateful for it. But I have a manor not far from here, with stores enough for a great company. We'll take ourselves there as we had meant to do before the storm blew us to your door, and give you back your peace."

Enid frowned. Averil thought she might object, but after a moment she shrugged. "You'll do as you will," she said. "Now please excuse me. I have work to do."

The others had already forgotten her. Mathilde's manor was a little less than a day's ride from this place in good weather. In the storm's aftermath, it might be longer. Mauritius and Riquier had their heads together, settling the when and the how, since the where was long since decided.

Averil did not try to stop them. They were perfectly right: they were straining this good woman's hospitality, and a farmstead was no fortress. Averil would be safer and better served in Gemigny.

She had no explanation for her unease, except that Gereint had left the house and so had Peredur, and she did not know where either of them was.

From the moment she came to know Gereint, she had been aware of him, where he was, what he did, as if he were a part of herself. Only the sorcerer's fog had been able to cut off that awareness.

There was no sorcery here. She searched for it in a kind of panic, but the false priest's workings were far away still. This was a different thing.

Gereint was still there. He was a twitching under the skin,

a roil of confusion in the heart. But that was all she knew. His thoughts and feelings that had been as clear to read as her own were gone.

It had not happened all at once. While she was distracted with Mathilde and Peredur and the vision of Gamelin, Gereint had softly and quietly drawn himself away. A wall rose between them now, a barrier so strong and high that she could neither scale it nor batter it down.

There was so much wrongness in the world, so much that was twisted or fallen out of true. Gereint should have been the one solid thing amid it all.

He still was. He must be.

Her allies were well engaged in their various duties. She could leave them to it for a while. She retrieved her mantle and went where Gereint would most likely go.

IT WAS LIKE a play on a stage. Gereint had confronted his long-lost father; now his mother appeared, with snow thick on her shoulders and an expression that boded well for none of them.

"You're all leaving tomorrow," she said, "and that's a good thing."

"For you, no doubt," Peredur said. "I am sorry."

"Are you? Are you capable of it?"

Gereint wondered that himself. Peredur said, "My mother was mortal. Sometimes I remember what it is to be one of you."

There was irony in that, and a touch of sadness.

Enid's lip curled. "Your father loved and left a woman, too, did he?"

"No," said Peredur. "That sin is entirely my own."

"I wish you wouldn't go to Gemigny," she said. It was abrupt, harsh, and rather unexpected. "I don't trust that woman. She rings false."

"She's a courtier," Peredur said. "They're all slightly hollow."

"Maybe so," said Enid, "but you'll be wise to find another prince's house to hide in."

Peredur shook his head. "There is none so close, and no castellan we can trust more than that one. We'll be on guard."

"You had better be," she said. "If anything happens to my son, I'll hunt you down. Do you understand?"

"Perfectly," said Peredur.

"You should come with us," Gereint said. "If the king's men come here—"

"You'd better stop them, hadn't you?" she said.

Any other woman would have been in tears, either railing at the man who had abandoned her or weeping on his neck. But not Enid. She was as strong as the armor Gereint had learned to wear, and hard, with no mercy in her.

She tossed each of them a pitchfork. "Horses don't stop passing manure just because the world is ending."

Peredur's brows rose. So did Gereint's. They were family, that gesture said—both of them.

It was not acceptance. It was certainly not forgiveness. But it warmed Gereint's heart nonetheless.

AVERIL LEANED AGAINST the wall. None of them was aware of her—even Gereint. And no wonder.

She should have seen it. It was obvious once one knew. Obvious, and in its way devastating.

He was more a child of Paladins than any noble alive. The blood ran strong and true, direct from the source.

And that meant . . .

No. He still could not marry. And she must. They were as star-crossed as they ever had been.

Now she understood where his magic came from and why it was what it was—and why and how he had tried to hide this from her. Wild magic had begotten him. Magic of the orders had not even existed when his father was born.

Gereint had brought his confusion to heel. Averil's was just beginning.

She had choices to make, but it seemed all power to choose had been taken from her. If she ran, where would she go? How could she face the world alone, without allies, without defenders?

The Rose was hers. Mathilde was not, but she belonged to the Isle. The Isle and the Rose had been allies from the beginning.

Within Averil, along the currents of her power, the web of the Rose shimmered as word passed from Knight to Knight and Squire to Squire. She recognized the spark that was Mauritius and that which was her oldest and most devoted ally, the Lord Protector of her duchy, the Knight Commander Bernardin.

Bernardin knew what Mauritius knew: that Lys was sore beset. He had the mortal army in his power, the court and the commons of the royal city, and at least a fraction of the orders—all that the late king had not corrupted.

Those noble warrior-mages agreed with Mathilde that the queen was best served if she remained in hiding. They would find and destroy the sorcerer. Her duty was to wait and pray and be ready to come forth when the victory was won. Then they would crown her.

Oh, indeed, they meant well. They revered, even loved her. They laid their lives and magic at her feet.

It seemed they had forgotten everything they knew of her—of Averil: not the duchess, not the queen, not the banner for the mustering of armies; Averil who was happier in a library than in a council chamber, who preferred a servant's gown to the silks and jewels of a queen, and who could ride and shoot rather well. Certainly they were not thinking of what else she was, of the magic she had that only Gereint shared—the Knights had never understood that, or seen the use in it.

Their blindness had brought Lys to this pass, and their failures had given the king his greatest victories. Now the king's sorcerer meant to carry on in his place.

The Rose had not destroyed the king. Gereint had, with Averil's power bolstering his. No one had celebrated him for it; they barely seemed to realize what he had done. As far as most of them knew or remembered, the sea had swallowed Clodovec and his black fleet.

That suited Gereint—he hated to put himself forward. And yet he should have. He was the best weapon they had.

The Knights were still disposing their forces as they saw best with their dim and blinkered sight. Averil gathered herself to speak, but when she had mustered the words, she let them die unspoken. She needed the strongest of arguments, so clear and compelling that none of them could fail to listen.

For that she needed Gereint, his power and the knowledge he hardly knew he had, and the lineage he was not yet ready to confess to. He was still holding himself apart from her, focused on his mother and on the father he had never expected to find.

She would give him a little time—a day. Until they came to Gemigny.

By then, who knew? Maybe the Knights had the right of it, and all of this would settle itself without her. Then she would take her throne and rule unchallenged, and Lys would find its soul again.

7

DISTRACTION IS A beautiful thing," said Gamelin. His ally stretched like a big sleek cat and dropped back gracefully onto the couch from which the sorcerer had roused him. "Indeed? Where's the beauty in distracting me from sleep?"

"You sleep more than enough already," Gamelin said.

Prince Esteban yawned with elaborate insolence. "I'm hoarding strength for the battle."

"We need you awake," said Gamelin. "Come, up. The enemy have opened their eyes at last, and seen what has risen to face them. The war has begun."

"So soon?"

"Some would say it's rather too late."

"He's truly dead, then," said Esteban: "Clodovec."

"Dead and sprouting sea-kelp from his emptied eyes." Gamelin hissed faintly. "With his grand designs, he failed us all."

"Did he, then? The Rose has returned to Lys. Will you wager that they've brought their god's great working—whatever it is—to its native land?"

"So they have done," said Gamelin, "in their arrogance and sacred folly."

The small hairs rose on Esteban's body. "Truly? The Mystery is here? The Great One's prison has come to us at last?"

Gamelin bent his head, then raised it: the briefest of nods.

"Then it's time," said Esteban. "Where is it? Tell me!"

"Soon," said Gamelin.

The man was a snake—truly. Esteban hissed at him, but he was not to be moved. He would keep his knowledge to himself until it suited his whim to reveal it.

That would not be long. All forces in heaven and earth were moving toward this great conclusion.

For the moment, he would be patient. He would play the false priest's game, and ride where he was bidden. But when the time came, Esteban would do no man's bidding.

THE SILENCE WAS deafening. After days of the wind's howling, morning dawned pale and calm. The sun rose with warmth it had not shown since winter began.

It was false warmth: there were months of winter yet to come. But for the moment it was a gift.

Averil's escort was packed and ready by sunrise. Her own packing had been quick and simple. Mathilde's was elaborate, as a lady's might be expected to be. As the sun rose in a startlingly clear sky, all of them were ready, horses saddled, men preparing to mount.

Enid had made herself scarce. Averil felt the hurt in Gereint, along with the understanding. What Peredur thought, there was no telling.

Those three had much to settle, come the time. Today they had other preoccupations.

In that deep snow, horses and men would need magic to pass, but to move that many required more power than was safe to venture. It would blaze like a beacon to any mage with the eyes to see.

The lesser working, to transform the snow into a track that would support them all, could conceal itself behind wards and, both Mauritius and Mathilde hoped, escape detection. Those of the Rose who had already left them would go on in hopes of luring the enemy astray. The company that had taken shelter in Enid's holding would ride for Gemigny.

It was all wise and careful, as it should be, since Knights had planned it. Averil had no useful objection to raise, particularly when it became clear that Peredur would join the diversion. He would make his way to Lutèce if he could, and help to bolster the defenses there—for they were all certain that if the enemy failed to find the queen on the road, he would turn toward the royal city.

Averil was not as sure of that as they, but she kept her head down and her tongue still. She had her own thoughts to think, and time to think them, too, in the blue-white cold and the sharp clean scent of snow. She wrapped herself tightly in warm wool and borrowed furs, and effaced herself among the escort.

Mathilde's guardsmen had sworn to protect the queen. They seemed honest men, and their souls were safe in their bodies. They were not mages, which served Averil's purpose.

The one gesture she allowed herself was a glance back as she rode away from the farmstead. It had been a surprisingly pleasant place, all things considered. She was almost sorry to leave it.

GEREINT KEPT HIS eyes fixed firmly on the road ahead, the flat and glimmering track that ran through hills and valleys deep-buried in snow. The land he had grown up in was changed beyond recognition.

It fit his mood. He had not said farewell to Peredur, nor did Peredur seek him out. There was too much to say; best to say nothing at all.

Half a day's silent, icy ride past the farmstead, long after Peredur had ridden away eastward, the snow dwindled abruptly into a more familiar winter landscape of browns and greys and deep green. The storm had barely brushed the hilltops here; an hour farther on, Gereint saw no snow at all. Though the cold still cut to the bone, the road was clear.

They stopped there to rest the horses and drink from a stream that was swift enough not to have turned to ice. As they paused, the web within pulsed, bringing Knight and Squires to the alert.

"Alain," said Riquier. He had a gift for recognizing the face of a man's magic, even far away and all but lost in sorcerous fog.

Alain's call was urgent but not desperate. He had found the sorcerer—Gereint had a distinct sense of serpents hissing. He was laying a trap, but his strength alone was not enough.

"I'll go," Riquier said.

"No," said Mauritius. "This needs a master's magic. Stay with the queen, both of you."

"Messire," Averil said. Even Gereint had not known that she was so close, or that she was listening. "What if the trap isn't Alain's but the sorcerer's? We can't afford to lose you."

"It is Alain," Mauritius said, "and the word he sends is truth. We can't afford to let him fail."

Gereint bit his lip so hard he tasted blood. Riquier spoke for both of them, and for Averil, too. "Our lady can't afford to lose any more of us."

"The two of you will keep her safe," Mauritius said as if she had not been standing there, glaring at him. "Stay with her; let nothing and no one draw you away."

"Don't do anything rash," said Averil.

Mauritius bent his head to her. "I'll come back to you, lady. I promise."

"You do that," she said.

Mauritius took the bag of bread and provisions that Gereint offered, and turned his horse's head east and north—toward Lutèce.

Gereint glanced at Averil. Her face was tight. But she did not command him to stop. Even the queen did not have that power, not over a Knight Commander of the Rose.

They watched until Mauritius had ridden out of sight over the hill. Then the escort bestirred itself, mounting and falling into place around the queen, preparing to escort her onward to Gemigny.

The wards were no weaker without Mauritius to sustain them. He had left the heart of his working with Mathilde, and she was a strong mage. Yet Gereint felt his absence keenly. The Knight had been his almost constant companion since he first came to the Rose.

He would come back soon enough, or they would come to him. In the meantime, Gereint and Riquier had a queen to look after. That was a great trust; between them they swore to be worthy of it.

They rode on toward Gemigny, alert for roving bands of king's men, but it seemed those had spared this country. The few travelers on the roads were ordinary farmers and tradesmen, and now and then a priest or a troop of monks traveling to church or abbey.

Mathilde's armed men sent the rest scrambling off the road. That was common enough among the gentry, but Gereint could not help but reflect that when Knights shared the road, there was always room for lesser folk to pass.

THE CLOSER THE escort drew to Gemigny, the more brightly intrusive Mathilde became. At first she honored Averil's evident desire to be left alone, but as the hours stretched and the road grew long, it seemed she no longer needed to devote her attention to maintaining the wards.

Averil had no art of courtly conversation. She had never felt it to be a lack: in her experience, if one said nothing and maintained a blandly pleasant expression, one's companions would more than fill the silence.

Mathilde seemed delighted to play the game. "You'll like Gemigny, I think," she said. "It's a very pretty town; its gardens are famous, though you'll see little of those in this season. It has a church of Ste. Genevieve with a healing spring, and a spire so tall that from the top of it you can see clear across the demesne. My manor sits outside it in a circle of fields and vineyards—our wine is the best I know of; the Lord Pope in Romagna has us send him a cask every autumn, and in return he sends us a jar of oil from his own olives, so golden and rich . . . ah! You'll taste it, lady, when you come to the manor."

Averil did not mean to listen to her prattle, but it was oddly seductive. It drew her out of her thoughts and scattered her focus.

"Thanks to the good God and my own arts," Mathilde said, "the past years' troubles have spared us. Our young men have kept their souls in their bodies, and our people have prospered. Our storehouses and granaries are full. You'll dine well at my table, and without guilt: there is no hunger in my demesne, and as little sorrow as there may be where human creatures are."

That was a great boast and a proud achievement. Averil should have found it comforting, but it only made her the more wary. Her duchy of Quitaine prospered, too, but that prosperity was hard-earned. This felt strange—it rang false, as Enid had said of Gemigny's lady.

All too often Averil caught her hand slipping toward the talisman that hung about her neck. It seemed heavier with each hour that passed, dragging her down with the weight of its secret.

For herself she cared little enough. If she died or was captured, Lys could find another queen. But if the thing she guarded fell into hostile hands, far more than Lys would suffer for it.

More than once on the road to Gemigny, the weight of that tiny, terrible thing kept her from bolting. For her own safety she cared little, but the Serpent's prison must not, now or ever, come near the Serpent's mage.

As she rode up the hill to the manor's gate, she turned her face toward the sky and the illusion of freedom with which it taunted her. The blue vault was empty even of birds. No creature of the wild magic danced there or anywhere in this rigidly ordered country.

That was not such an ill thing. If wild magic could not come here, Serpent magic might find its way difficult as well.

GEMIGNY'S CASTLE WAS very old. Its heart had housed a princely farmer when Romagna ruled this part of the world. Now that Romagna was gone, sundered into a dozen squabbling kingdoms, the villa on the hilltop had grown a wall of stone and a quartet of creneled towers. But inside it was still a villa rather than a castle, with its square of rooms and halls around an open court, and its retinue of outbuildings.

In another time, in other company, Averil would have found it charming. The court was a garden with a little orchard and a pool gone glassy with ice; the floors in the rooms to which she was led by silently gracious servants were blissfully warm. Here as seldom in this aging world, the hypocaust still worked its magic, warming the house from beneath.

This could be a pleasant place to hide while her servants won back her kingdom. After the war was over, maybe she would come back and do the manor justice. Tonight she al-

lowed herself to accept the bath and the clean and freshly
scented garments which Mathilde's maids offered her.

Magic wove through all of this place, caught in the glass
of the tesserae, but it was old magic, worn thin with age.
The windows were clear and empty of power; there were no
workings apart from the mosaics, no signs that this place
belonged to a mage. Wherever Mathilde kept the trappings
of her calling, it was not here.

There were wards—strong ones, so strong they made
Averil's head ache. But they were outside, set on the wall that
surrounded the manor. The manor itself was open, empty,
unguarded.

She was sure that it was meant to give her comfort. If her
magic had been purely of the orders, she would have been
glad of the peace within, and barely noticed the strength of
the protections that shielded her from the enemy's sorcery.
She could see in Riquier, as he rode through the gate, how
the tightness left his body and his face lost a little of the haggard look that had beset them all since they came to Lys.

For him this was a place of rest, of quiet and of ordered
peace. For Averil with her taint of wild magic, it was almost
unbearable.

Gereint must find it at least as distressing as she did. She
could not tell. He was in the manor: he had gone with the
rest of the men to what must be a guardroom. But the
buzzing of the wards and the division that had grown between them kept her from sensing any more than that.

The web of the Rose was gone from inside her. The
wards kept it out as they did all other magic. When she

reached for it, the wards' buzzing rose to a shriek. She recoiled, half blind with pain.

More wrongness. It infected everything here, wherever she turned. It was not exactly like the fog that surrounded the sorcerer's workings; it was accidental, surely, an unintended consequence of the mingled magics in this place. And yet it was just as virulent and just as destructive to her mind and magic.

She had never been more alone than she was now. Servants waited on her, smiling warmly, seeming delighted with the task, but they were strangers. All of her men of the Rose were gone but two, and they were separated from her.

She could call to Gereint and he would come. Even from the borders of death, he would do that.

But she restrained herself. In this place, in the solitude of her mind, she faced a cold truth.

This thing between them, this one soul in two bodies, had always seemed to make her stronger. And yet did it really? Or did it make both of them more vulnerable?

She struggled to live without him, to be herself outside of his thoughts, his mind and heart. Her magic was a shadow of itself. It kept reaching for the place where he should be, where the wall was that he had raised—and now the wards on this manor drove them even farther apart.

She could force the wall down. It was as simple as standing in front of him and telling him he had nothing to hide—she knew what he was.

Yet should she? Or should she let the bond between them wither, for both their sakes?

She could not make the choice tonight. Instead she played the polite and obliging guest. She dined in the hall with its glimmering mosaics and faded tapestries, made conversation with Mathilde, and kept the corner of her eye on the lower table where the two Squires sat.

They seemed at ease. A handful of Mathilde's young men sat with them, warm with wine and laughter.

Riquier matched them cup for cup, or seemed to. Gereint never touched his, but he smiled and jested with the rest of them.

He was in no pain. No danger, either, it seemed. For that, whatever else she might be feeling, Averil breathed a fraction easier. But she did not let down her guard.

THE NIGHT WAS too quiet.

With so much else to fret over, the absence of either wildfolk or birds had seemed a trivial thing. But as the long winter's night stretched toward the late and frozen dawn, Gereint tossed on his borrowed pallet.

There was human noise enough here, snores and coughing and, off in a corner, the rhythmic grunting of a guard and a servant doing their best to shorten the night. But the world outside was utterly still. Not even a breath of wind blew.

Gereint had seen a wave gather in the sea, when the water drew far away from the glistening sand, falling back and back until it seemed all water would drain from the world—and then the deluge came, the wave as tall as a ship's mast, sweeping over the dry land, shattering all before it.

This night felt like that: like the empty shore with shells

scattered on it, bits of weed and wrack, and here and there a fish flopping helplessly, gasping in the alien air.

The wave was coming.

He rose softly from the pallet. Riquier, on the one beside him, muttered and burrowed into his blanket. If he felt what Gereint felt, he was not letting it rob him of sleep.

Gereint pulled on his boots and shook out his mantle, slipping it over his shoulders. Deep inside, so deep he could barely feel her, Averil was asleep, as the rest of them were.

He paused, doubling up with something very like pain. He had not meant to cut her off. He only wanted to work his slow way through the fact of what he was; to understand what it meant that he, the farmer's son, the godborn child, was half a Paladin.

She must think he had turned against her. She had not said anything, but that had its own significance. Averil could say more with silence than their noble host had said in a whole flood of words.

In the morning he would open his mind and magic to her, and both of them would be whole again. Tonight, there was this thing that he must do.

She was safe here. Gereint would not be gone long. Just long enough to find the heart of the silence.

THE MANOR'S WARDS were harder to pass than others he had met. They were out of joint like everything else here, tearing at him like thorns. But his magic was armor of a sort. It found a way through the thicket, out into the starlight.

The silence broke. The wave crashed down.

8

GEREINT WOKE TO the roar of the sea.

His head was pounding, and his stomach heaved. He lurched upward and flung himself sidewise before he emptied his guts on his own shirt.

Empty, still retching, he dragged himself upright. He was braced for the lurch and sway of a ship's deck, but the sea was gone, if it had ever been anywhere but in his head. Silver-white columns rose above him like trees of stone, branching into a vault high overhead.

He stood on solid earth and shaped stone, in a place that from the smell and the feel of it was both ancient and holy. Strict orders of magic bound it, but wild magic surged beneath, fiercely, marvelously alive.

Magic surrounded him. Only slowly did his eyes dull enough to see the bodies it wore. They were all women, all dressed in white or grey, ladies of great power both rooted in earth and soaring to heaven.

He had seen a Lady of the Isle before: the queen of Prydain was of that order, and both Averil and Mathilde had been acolytes. These were like them. They were old and young and in between, but they all had the same magic.

He turned completely about, taking his time, marking each face and the light of power that wore that face like a mask. When he had come back to the first, whose face was the oldest, he stopped.

"You're not afraid of us." That was the Lady beside the eldest. She was not young, exactly, but not old, either. She seemed more bemused than surprised.

"Should I be?" he asked.

"Most men would be," the eldest Lady said. She was smiling, but her eyes were steady, deep and, he had to admit, rather alarmingly keen.

He could see why they might expect him to be terrified. "If you wanted me dead or worse," he said, "I wouldn't be awake or able to see your faces."

"You should not be," another of the Ladies said. Unlike the first two, she seemed perturbed, even angry. "What are you? Tell us!"

Gereint's finger brushed the silver rose over his heart. "You see what I am. I'm a Squire of the Rose. Am I on the Isle? Was I supposed to stumble into your trap?"

"We laid it for a Knight," the angry Lady said. The others hissed at her, but she glared them down. "What difference does it make? He's not what we cast the net for. Work the spell, take away his memory, fling him back and seize another while there's still time."

"I think not," the eldest said.

Gereint shivered slightly. The sickness that had gripped him was gone, but the wariness had grown. All his life, he had been taught to revere the Ladies and the Isle. They defended the high magic, they protected the Young God's children, they guarded their secrets while the brothers of the Rose fought the world's wars.

The Rose was the hand, the Isle the heart. Or so everyone said.

Gereint found no warmth here, and certainly no sisterly feeling.

"Tell us," the eldest Lady said to him. "What do you know of the Mysteries?"

Gereint's heart stilled. "Far less than you, I'm sure, Lady," he said.

"Perhaps," she said. "But with the Rose so sorely tried, and so many lost, knowledge is gone, too, and arts, and the workings of years. Tell us, messire, what you know."

"Lady," said Gereint, "I'm but a Squire. The Knight Commanders and the Lord Protector know all that's left to know."

"There is nothing left," said the Lady who stood beside the eldest. "The Mysteries are gone—whether taken or destroyed, none of us knows."

Some of the others hissed at her as if she betrayed secrets, but she took no notice. Her eyes on Gereint were wise and kind.

He wanted to trust her, but that could be a trap, too. He could not imagine for what good reason a circle of Ladies might cast a snare to catch a Knight. They should be able to simply go to Mauritius or Bernardin or any of the others, and ask.

If they had, and if they had got no answer, then it was

not Gereint's place to give them one. He met them with his most obtuse expression, gave them the bullock-brained farm lad he had never honestly been—but these were gentry. They knew no better. "The Mysteries," he said—"that's the Young God's shroud and his spear, yes? Squires aren't taught anything about them, except what they are. But I heard they're gone now. When the Rose fell, they fell, too."

"So we heard," the Lady said. "And yet, you are here. The magic was precise; it should have drawn in one who knows."

Gereint had no need to feign his guilt, or to lie, either. "That's my fault, then, Lady. I couldn't sleep, you see. The world's so strange now. I was out wandering; I must have fallen into the working. I am sorry. I hope I haven't done any harm."

"No more than anyone else has," the eldest Lady said somewhat wearily. "Yes, the world is strange, and magic is no longer the clear and ordered thing that it was. Go back to your bed, messire."

There was magic in the words, a spell that tried to muddle his mind—and so it might have, if his magic had been a clear and ordered thing. He mustered the wits to go all slack-jawed and loose-kneed; when the net bound him, he did not try to fight it.

He left part of himself outside the net, a tiny moth of a spell, all ears and gauzy wings. It heard what it needed to hear.

"Folly," the angry Lady said. "Folly and stupidity. Surely it cannot be that no man of the Rose knows where the Mystery is. One of them does. One of them must."

"Unless it's sunk to the bottom of the sea," said one whom Gereint had not heard before. "If Clodovec had it with him when he sailed against the Isle—"

"He sailed against Prydain," said the Lady with the kind voice. "Not the Isle. What is in Prydain, that he would have been seeking?"

"The remnant of the Rose," the angry Lady said. "Which must still keep the Mystery, if—"

"Unless there is more in Prydain than we know of," the kind Lady said.

She was righter maybe than she knew. Gereint struggled to stay, to hear more, but the magic had stretched thin. Ladies and hall whirled away, and his consciousness with it.

GEREINT DID NOT know this bed he woke in, nor the ceiling over it or the walls around it. The face above him he did know: Ademar, frowning as if he presented a conundrum that the Novice had been ordered to solve.

He lurched upright. "God in heaven! This isn't Gemigny."

"Not even close," said Ademar. "What are you doing in Lutèce?"

"I could ask the same of you," Gereint said.

"The Myrddin," said Ademar.

Of course it would be Peredur, the Myrddin of Prydain, who brought the Novice five days' fast journey in a night. "Is it just you? Or—"

"Mauritius is here," Ademar said.

"Alain?"

The Novice's face went somber. He shook his head. "You

were right, Mauritius said. It was a false trail. It led to a nest of sorcerer's slaves, and Alain was in it. He had—been—"

Even the bold and insouciant Ademar could not say the words. Gereint spared him the necessity—after a fashion. "How many others?"

"Only Alain," said Ademar. He drew a deep breath. "The Lord Protector has called the others in. It's too dangerous for them to be abroad in ones and twos. He's mounting armies, as much as he can, and sending them against the king's men."

"There are men left in Lys with souls and bodily strength to fight?" Gereint asked.

"There are a few," said Ademar. "Come, you're wanted. Mauritius is waiting."

HE WAS INDEED, though Peredur was not. He stood with the Lord Protector in a remarkably crowded garrison, inspecting an armed company.

Only a few looked like men of Lys. The rest must have come from Gotha or Moresca, fair men and dark with a different cast to the face than Gereint had seen in his own country or in Prydain.

They did not have the look of mercenaries, either, as far as Gereint had ever known. These must be free allies, brave men and strong arrayed against the Serpent's slaves.

Gereint bent his head to the Knights, then stood at attention while Bernardin gave them their orders. They were to ride southward, find a nest of soulless near a town called

Charteret, and destroy it. "And if they melt into mist and shadow, as so many have before," he said, "trust the Squire who rides with you to hunt them to their lair."

Gereint did not recognize the man in the blue cotte who waited with the rest. He was older than Squires were wont to be, but the weight of his magic was almost substantial enough to be a Knight's. He yielded pride of place to the Gothan who wore the captain's tabard, with an air that proclaimed both intelligence and good sense.

That was a man worth studying. His glance met Gereint's as he marched out of the barracks, measuring him quickly and raising a brow at the youth and strength of him. They parted without a word spoken or a name exchanged, in mutual respect.

In the silence and sudden emptiness of the barracks, Gereint faced his Knight Commander as was proper, and addressed him. "Messire," he said.

"Messire," Mauritius said in return. "You have a tale to tell, I think."

Gereint could do better than tell it. He showed it, calling on the air to make a mirror, and in the mirror all that he had done and seen since he went wandering from his bed in Gemigny.

After he had begun the working, he caught Bernardin's eye. There was a distinctly sardonic glint there.

Gereint was being impertinent—again. He should have asked for a glass, and asked one of the Knights to work the magic.

Neither of them wasted time in rebuking him. They

were intent on the scene that played before them, reading more in each word and gesture than Gereint in his ignorance was capable of.

When the last of it was done, when the vision had melted into lamplight, Gereint was ready to bow and retreat, but Mauritius held up a hand. "Stay."

Gereint was bound to obedience. He was not bidden to sit, which left him standing while the Knights sat together on a bench to ponder in silence. It was punishment of a sort.

He held tightly to patience. Every moment he spent here, he was not in Gemigny, watching over Averil. The Ladies had made a natural mistake, and it served him well enough. But time was running on.

There was no pressing the Knights. The web that bound the Rose was humming. The Isle had moved at last, and not against their enemies.

Throughout this war, the Ladies had guarded themselves without regard for their brothers. When the Rose fell in Lys, the Isle had done nothing. It had been Prydain that gave the remnants sanctuary, while the Isle raised walls of air against any who came near.

"What game are they playing?" Mauritius asked.

He did not expect an answer, and Gereint had none.

Bernardin sat motionless, chin on breast, but there was nothing resembling sleep in his posture. He was the oldest of the Knights who still lived, and he had stayed alone in Lys when the rest of the Rose fled. As Lord Protector of Quitaine he had defended his lady's duchy while she lived in exile; now he protected her throne in Lutèce until she could come to claim it.

When he spoke, even Mauritius snapped to attention. "That was not the Isle to which our Squire was taken; it was the Ladies' Chapel here in our own cathedral. There is no mistaking it. And those whom we took for Ladies . . ."

"They were Ladies," Gereint said, speaking out of turn, but he could not keep silent. "Not all or even most, but the oldest and the one beside her, with a handful of others, had the full power. Most of the rest were acolytes."

"Yes," said Bernardin. "They send acolytes from the Isle to marry among the great families, or to lay claim to noble domains as my lady did. But the Ladies themselves only leave the Isle for strong cause."

"Such as a king who is trying to wake the Serpent, and the destruction of a kingdom, and the fall of the Rose?"

Gereint had gone beyond impertinence. He ducked his head and set his teeth together and vowed to himself to say no more.

"Such as all of those things," Mauritius said. "There is no trust left in the world, it seems."

"Nor has there been since I can remember," said Bernardin. "Well before Clodovec was born, the Rose and the Isle had drawn apart. They no longer shared secrets. The Isle turned inward, and the Rose devoted itself to its wars and its intrigues. Now when they would best profit from their old alliance, there's none to be had."

Gereint bit his tongue. Someone else would say it. Mauritius would, surely. But the others were silent.

"There must be something left," he said in a burst of desperation. "Shouldn't we stretch out a hand? Offer them what they're craving to know?"

"You had that chance," Mauritius said. "You refused it."

"It wasn't my place," said Gereint.

"Now you remember that?" said Mauritius. He did not seem angry—he never did. "No, no; you did well. Whatever the Ladies want or need of us, it's best they ask openly, not through spells and sleights of magic."

"We know what they want, messire," Gereint said. "They laid their trap for someone who knows where the great Mystery is. Shouldn't one of them have that knowledge, too?"

"One of them does," Bernardin said, "though she is but an acolyte—as you are but a Squire."

Gereint's teeth clicked together. He had been coming round to that thought, but it struck harder, somehow, to hear the Lord Protector say it. "Doesn't that seem wrong to you, messire? The old order of things is broken. What if there's no way to mend it?"

"We have to pray there is," said Mauritius, "or we're all lost."

"Are you going to approach the Ladies?" Gereint asked.

"Do you think we should?"

That set Gereint back on his heels. "I, messire? Does it matter what I think?"

"I believe it does," said his Knight Commander. "Do you?"

"I don't know," Gereint said. "I know so little of all these wars and politics. Princes and courtiers are altogether alien to me."

"Your heart knows," Bernardin said. "What does it tell you?"

"It tells me . . ." Gereint trailed off. "I don't know what it tells me. All I know is that I shouldn't be here. I should—I need to—be in Gemigny."

The Lord Protector spread his hands in what seemed to be honest regret. "That, messire, is not possible. The magic that brought you here is none of ours. The magic that transported Mauritius and the rest has gone about its business. War is rising; the enemy closes in. We can spare no more. Our lady is as well protected as she can be. We shall all have to be content with that."

Gereint's jaw set. Contentment was the farthest thing from his mind. "You've left her alone with a single Squire and no defenses. Are you the ones I should be fighting? Are you her enemies, too?"

"She has an acolyte of the Isle and a small army to defend her," said Bernardin, "and her own arts and magic, which are considerable. She is hardly alone."

Gereint shook his head. "No. No and no. You don't understand. She has arts and skill and strength, too—but never as much as when she has me. I make her strong, messire. If I'm not there—"

Both Knights were set against him, their minds closed, their eyes blind. "The lady and the Squire will give her their strength," Bernardin said. "You can be of use here. Go now, rest. In the morning you'll be assigned duties."

Gereint opened his mouth to protest, but Mauritius overrode him. "You'll see her again soon enough, messire. The moment it's safe, we'll bring her here. That we promise you."

He was a wise man, and kind in his way. But he could

not see. None of them could. This whole world was blind to everything but itself.

Wise fools—they thought they bound him with obedience, with the oaths he had sworn. But the first and greatest of them all was to defend the world against the Serpent's servants.

Averil was the best hope they had. He bowed his head and shut his mouth and let himself be dismissed.

But when he came to the room in which he had slept, he had his magic all gathered and his spirit ready. He remembered the way of it, like slipping through wards: around, and inabout. It was a simple thing, as the greatest workings were. He had only to reach, wish, be there—back in her blessed presence again.

Fog enveloped him. Emptiness gaped before him. Where she should have been was a wall of nothingness.

It was his imagination purely that heard laughter in the void. The Ladies had brought him here for their own blind and selfish purposes—not even knowing what they summoned. But the enemy knew. They had played directly into his hands.

There was no way back to Gemigny. The roads were barred in every world.

For once in his life, Gereint welcomed the eruption of magic inside him. He was almost a mage now: he could not stop it, but he could direct it. He flung the full force of it against the sorcerer's wall.

It swallowed that blast as it had all else. Gereint stood alone in the room, cold and shaking and for once empty of magic.

He could burst into tears. Or he could lie down and stare at the ceiling, and appreciate the irony of his position.

He would find his way back to her. He did not know how yet, or when, but he would do it. That oath he swore to himself, and held as sacred as his service to the Rose.

9

GEREINT WAS GONE. The sorcerer's fog had risen between them once more, overlaid with a peculiar sense, somewhat like blown glass and somewhat like the sea. If Averil could have named it, she would have said that it reminded her of the Isle.

He was nowhere in Gemigny, in manor or town. She could not tell where he was at all.

She held panic rigidly at bay. He was alive. That much, and that much only, she was sure of. She had to pray that he was safe.

Likewise she had to hold herself together. If this was an attack, she could not let it succeed. She had to be strong.

Dawn was just touching the sky as she rose and dressed. The manor still slept, mostly; the cooks were up, baking the morning's bread. She had in mind to coax a loaf or two out of them, but first she meant to find Riquier.

It was time to leave. Without Gereint, she could not trust that she would be safe, but the elder Squire was no feeble man, either. He had his own strong share of magic, and art and skill that rivaled hers.

There were guards on her door, not to keep her prisoner, they insisted with all courtesy, but to protect her from harm. There were wards, too, that brought Mathilde and another handful of armed and scrupulously polite men when Averil mustered the magic to pass.

They were all polite, smiling and bowing and expressing sincere concern for her safety. Averil resisted the impulse to blast them where they stood. She was not that far gone, yet.

Guest or prisoner, she was going nowhere this morning but where her avowedly loyal servants allowed her to go. That was to breakfast, then to the solar where Mathilde offered needlework and a player on a lute and a suitably edifying volume with a painfully shy young clerk to read it.

If there had been a library to escape to, Averil would have turned eagerly toward it. But the only books here, apart from the lives of unspeakably dull saints, were the manor's accounts and the rolls of its vassals.

That was a miscalculation, but a useful one. It allowed her to test a growing conviction.

"Is there a convent nearby?" she asked as the morning stretched interminably, "or a monastery with a library and an understanding abbot? I do love to read, you see, and I'm very poor at waiting, or at being waited on."

Mathilde started slightly. She had been engrossed in her embroidery, or else in the life and travails of yet another virgin martyr: Averil had not been paying attention, to know which. "Oh! Oh. Yes. No, there's no convent within a day's ride. There is an abbey, but I'm not sure—"

"Shall we pay it a visit?" Averil said. She did not care if she sounded excessively eager.

"It's not safe," Mathilde said. "Lady, you know what's on the roads. We can't risk—"

"It's not far, is it?" Averil interrupted her. "I thought I saw its tower when we rode through the town. With your men to guard me, I'll be in no danger, surely."

"It's too dangerous," said Mathilde. "I am sorry, lady, but I promised I'd protect you. Lys needs its queen."

"The queen of Lys needs her sanity," Averil said. "Your hospitality is most generous, and I do thank you for it, but I'm not made to live in a cage, even one as lovely as this. If I can't travel to my city, let me at least find entertainment for my restless mind—and a little for my body as well. I know your demesne is safe; no ill thing trespasses here. Or am I a prisoner after all?"

"No!" Mathilde said a little too quickly. "No, lady. Please, it's not wise. I'll send to the abbey if you like, and if you'll tell them what you would like to read. They'll be more than happy to oblige you."

Averil drew herself up to renew the fight, but after a moment's thought she subsided—not willingly, and not for long. But this needed subtlety.

"That is kind of you, lady," she said after a pause. "I would welcome whatever the good brothers can spare."

"It's done, then," Mathilde said.

She offered no escape from the hall, and no relief from the tedium of a noble lady's morning. But when Averil retreated to the kitchens, Mathilde neither followed nor tried to stop her. The ubiquitous guards dogged her steps, but it seemed she was allowed to wander a little after all, however briefly and on however short a leash.

Since she was a child on the Isle, Averil had been more at ease in the kitchen than in the ladies' solar. She found something close to contentment there now, kneading bread and scouring pots and turning the spit. In that humble labor, she had time to think, and to make such plans as she could.

First, escape this place. Then find Gereint. With his strength she had hope of winning this war.

She watched and waited and kept her counsel. And she listened, because servants knew everything.

They were expecting a guest. Their lady had forbidden them to lay on a feast, but there was more bread to bake than usual, and more fowl roasting on the spit. Some of those had come in with the guest's messenger, hunted on the road for the day's dinner.

The servants could not or would not tell Averil who it was. It was a mage, that much she could tell, and his coming was not only expected but long awaited.

It was not Gamelin. She asked the undercook, straight to his face. "Tell me. Is it the late king's priest?"

The man stared at her as if she had gone daft. "I'm sure I don't know, my lady."

"Then, sir, is it someone I know? Should I be prepared to welcome a friend?"

The undercook spread his hands. "Lady, these high matters are far beyond me. I only know that there's bread to finish and a subtlety to make."

That was as polite a dismissal as she had seen in a king's court. Averil had sense enough to let be.

The peace that had briefly blessed her was gone. She finished the last round of bread, pummeled it into shape, and laid it in the oven with the rest. She washed her hands in the pail by the hearth, where the water was almost warm, dried them, and put off her apron and slipped out of the kitchen.

RIQUIER WAS NOT in the guardroom, nor was he in the stable. None of the guards professed to have seen him.

Averil's hackles rose. There might be a perfectly reasonable explanation for the disappearance of one Squire of the Rose on the eve of an illustrious guest's arrival in Gemigny, but two?

Without Gereint she was not strong enough to elude the wards or slip through the wall between worlds. The wild magic could not come here, nor could she reach out to it through all the manor's defenses.

She had found that more pleasant than not, when she first came; wild magic made her skin creep. But it was her greatest strength and her best protection.

Gereint would have been proud that she finally admitted it. Magic of the orders was only the smallest part of what she was. She was everything she had been raised to fear, loathe, shun—all of those and more.

The stable was no sanctuary. Mathilde's guards surrounded her. If she made the slightest move toward horse or saddle, an armed man stood in the way. Usually he smiled. But he would not step aside even for a direct command.

There was more to this than an avowed determination to keep the queen safe. She would not say, yet, that it stank of Serpent magic. But it was all just a little too obsessive.

She left the stable and retreated to the chapel. The Church encompassed all that made the orders so deadly to wild magic: rigid restraint, hidebound ritual, pure blindness to any power but its own. And yet, as Averil knelt in front of the altar in its shroud of winter white, the light through clear and unmagical windows bathed her face.

It was pure light, untainted by enchantment. There was no magic here. There should have been tangled skeins of it, spell upon spell, built through the ages since this manor's lord owed allegiance to the emperor of Romagna.

Someone had cleansed this place, scoured it clean and left it open to the powers of earth and air. It offered no defense, nor did it open a way for her escape, but it freed her magic to raise its own walls and strong protections.

A shadow veiled the sun. Averil swayed, caught in midworking. A breath hissed past her ear; she thought she heard the slither of scales. Glimmering walls of magic rose around her.

She bowed to the altar and turned slowly. Mathilde stood watching her, with a handful of maids and guards, and a man with an all-too-familiar face.

Prince Esteban of Moresca had sued for her hand while she played the game of courts and palaces in Lutèce. She had come perilously close to accepting him, though he was one of the Serpent's servants and a master of magics that should long since have died from the world.

He was a prince, a child of Paladins, and a most charming and persuasive companion. His smile was as warm as she remembered, with the slight edge of danger that made her belly quiver. He seemed truly glad to see her.

So he should be: she was neatly and inescapably trapped. From the vantage of this chapel and this moment, she saw each step that had led her here, each shard of betrayal, measured in each Knight and Squire and Novice of the Rose who had been separated from her until she was trapped, alone, in this place.

By now it was no surprise, yet it struck her with a faint but distinct shock. She, like any fool, had hoped to the last that her instincts were false.

"My lord," she said to Esteban.

As she rose from her knees, he sank to his, bowing with grace and no perceptible hint of mockery. "Majesty," he said.

He reached for her hand and kissed it. She stiffened, but had the presence of mind not to pull away. He smiled up at her, his dark eyes glinting, the keenly carved face with its impeccable beard offering its beauty as a gift.

That was a spell, and a clever one: half seduction, half glamour. She should study it, when there was time. A queen could well use such a working.

"So, my lord," she said. "Have you come to take my soul?"

"I'll steal your heart, lady," said Esteban, "but your soul is yours to keep."

"Ah," she said. "It's only young men you take, and only the strongest, to build your armies."

He shook his head and shuddered slightly. "That's no magic of mine, majesty."

"But it serves your purpose."

She well remembered that slight shrug, that lift of a

shoulder and that tilt of a brow. "In war, we take what weapons we can."

"And now you have the queen," she said.

"I hope she may join us willingly," said Esteban.

"Indeed? Why would I do that?"

"To save your people," he said. "To take and hold your kingdom as you were born to do. The old ways are failing—surely you see that as clearly as I. It's time a new order rose in the world."

"A new order? Or one so old it's new again?"

"Does it matter?"

"Probably not," she said. "What if I refuse?"

He flowed smoothly to his feet. She had forgotten how tall he was. Not as tall as Gereint, but tall enough, lightly built and strong like a steel blade. "I think, majesty, that you will come round to our way of thinking." He held out his hand and bowed again, less deeply now, still smiling. "Will you come?"

Averil stood still. The chapel was a sanctuary, but it offered little shelter, no food or water, and no mortal help. The sky without was empty of wildfolk. It would be a cold and lonely vigil if she insisted on keeping it.

She ignored his hand and waited pointedly for him to lead her wherever he meant to go.

He seemed undismayed, and certainly not crestfallen. He lowered his hand. When she declined to be herded like a sheep, he sighed faintly and led as she commanded him.

Mathilde, Averil was unbecomingly pleased to see, was visibly unhappy. Averil refused to acknowledge her at all, to speak or offer courtesy.

Esteban was an honest enemy. Mathilde was a much lower order of being: the traitor who wore the face of a friend.

Averil felt nothing yet—no anger, no fear. She was keenly aware of everything and everyone that surrounded her. She came close more than once to asking where her Squires were, but if they had escaped, she knew better than to betray them.

She prayed instead that at least one of them would find his way to Lutèce. The sooner the Knights knew what had happened, the better for them all.

10

THE SNAKE WAS no thicker than Esteban's smallest finger, and no longer than his forearm. It was dull brown like fallen leaves, but with the shimmer on its scales that every snake had, as if in tribute to the great Serpent that was the father of them all.

In certain lights, Gamelin's cheeks and forehead and his tonsured crown had the same subtle gleam. That he was not human, or not entirely so, Esteban had long since concluded.

This small and deadly snake coiled peacefully around the priest's narrow wrist. Its head rested in his palm, tongue flicking, tasting the air.

The man in the chair watched it with eyes that had gone past fear. If any expression remained in them, it was hope— for a clean death, however painful.

He was hardly more than a boy, a compactly graceful young man with smooth brown skin and curling black hair. Lys was full of his like; its nobility produced them in litters like puppies. But even the sons of Paladins were not often as strong in magic as this one was.

His body was intact. Gamelin never stooped to breaking bones. He broke the mind instead, and undid the magic, spell by spell, until in the end he plucked the soul from the emptied husk and crushed it into nothingness.

This one still had his soul and most of his sanity. His magic was a dimming ember.

Gamelin cradled the serpent, stroking its head absently, in no fear of its poison. "So, messire," he said. "Tell us again what lies in Prydain, that its queen defends so valiantly."

The captive set his lips together. He had said no word yet, but the priest's spell wound through his mind. Shards of awareness flashed through the globe of crystal that hung before his eyes.

In the beginning the globe had turned slowly, and little had shown in it but sparks of light and now and then what must be a memory: a dance with swords, a woman's face, a garden of blood-red roses. Little by little, as Gamelin's spell did its work, the globe spun more swiftly.

Now it was a dizzying sphere of light. Memories spun from it, darting past like sparks from a fire.

Not all or even most were the boy's memories. A web of light bound him to a world of knowledge, a structure of magic that encompassed the whole of an order. It could be he did not even know what he knew—but Gamelin would find it. He would delve to the heart of all the Mysteries which this Squire of the Rose was sworn to protect.

When Gamelin spoke, the sparks drew together into shapes that Esteban could sometimes make sense of. As often as not, they scattered again, dissolving into incoherence.

That was the prisoner fighting the spell. He was strong;

he had fought well. But he was losing the fight. Out of the confusion of visions, Esteban plucked a handful that might, in their way, yield an answer.

A forest of trees with leaves that rattled strangely, like scales. A circular chamber with niches in its walls, and in each niche, a heap of dust and crumbling bones. The rattle of scales again, raining down on a field of dead and dying. Ships on the sea, and a far green shore, and a lady crowned with light.

"Yes," said Gamelin, a long, soft hiss. "Yessss . . ."

The prisoner began to struggle, battling the bonds that held him.

Gamelin held the snake close to the prisoner's face. "This you may have, messire, if you will tell us. Where is it? Where is the key?"

The dark eyes fixed on that hope of release. The blur of memories slowed. Roses bloomed like a spill of blood.

He flung himself forward onto Gamelin. The serpent struck with blinding speed, sinking its fangs in his cheek.

His body convulsed, and yet he smiled. His eyes laughed as he fell down into death. He still had his soul and his order's secret, for all that his enemies could do.

GAMELIN ROSE STIFFLY from beneath the slack body. He too was smiling. There was a cord in his hand, insubstantial as a spider's thread. It coiled through the dead man's eyes and bound itself to the web within, that working too complex for any one mind to encompass.

It was fading fast. Gamelin's cord tugged at it, even as it unraveled, collapsing on itself.

The sorcerer swayed. For a moment he seemed even less human than before. His cheeks had gone pallid green.

Still his eyes gleamed with a kind of triumph. "That was a brave child, but no mortal may hide the truth from me. It is contained in the web, in the knowledge of his order. The woman holds the Mystery."

Esteban's heart quickened. "The woman? The queen?"

"Your quarry, my lord," said Gamelin.

Esteban swept a bow. His ally had no humor, and no understanding of bravura, either. "Dispose of this," he said to the hulk of a soldier who stood by the wall.

The creature did his bidding silently, as all the soulless did. It lifted the body and carried it away—to what fate, Esteban would not inquire too closely.

Some necessities were more evil than others. Esteban would be glad when he no longer needed this one. But for the moment, he did need both the sorcerer and his armies. Come the Unbinding, when the world was transformed, that, too, would change.

AVERIL FOUND THE solar even less congenial now than before she became a prisoner in it, but one thing she could say for it: she was no longer bored. She sat by the fire with her hands folded in her lap, ignoring the maid who read from the unspeakably dull book and the servants who tried to ply with her with wine. When they offered food, she took a little of that, but carefully, lest it be poisoned.

As far as she could tell, it was not. Esteban had bowed her into the room and then left her, striding off on some urgent errand. She moved to send a thread of magic in pursuit, but none came to her hand.

Her body's senses were preternaturally alert, but her magic was dull and distant. When she reached for it, it slid away.

Clever captors, to separate her first from her Squires and then from her magic. It was a subtle spell; it emptied her as it had emptied the chapel, and poured her magic, slowly but inescapably, into the wards that guarded the manor.

Even yet, fear barely touched her. She had her wits still, and her soul was secure in her body. She would do what she could with those.

The pendant hung heavy on her breast. She had long since trained herself not to touch it, to draw no attention to it at all. Apart from herself and Gereint, four people in the world knew what she had: Peredur, the queen of Prydain and her Knight Commander of the Rose, and Mauritius. None of them was here, or would betray her.

She schooled herself to breathe slowly and deeply; she willed the tension out of her shoulders and back. Old exercises from the Isle served her now in good stead, skills of the mind and body that allowed her to rest but prepared her for whatever might come.

Even with all of that, when the blow struck, she reeled almost into darkness. A gasp escaped her, the whisper of a name: "Riquier!"

She felt him die. She felt his gladness, his surety that he had won the battle. And she felt the sorcery that pierced the web of the Rose in the moment of his passing.

For a blinding instant she had it back, all of it, free of fog and the buzzing of wards—even Gereint, even the half of herself. Then it rent asunder. Workings shattered; minds bent or broke.

With the last of the power that was left to her, Averil dived into the fog. It was a mad thing, a hopeless thing, but worse by far would have been to go down in the ruin of the web.

She sat in echoing silence, truly and utterly alone. Too large a part of her thrashed in agony. Grimly she quelled it.

She could grieve for Riquier, because it filled her mind and heart with something—anything. She wept without shame or restraint. He had been a friend, an ally, a teacher. She had loved him as a brother.

Fear stabbed at last, to the heart. Gereint—dear God, if they had him, too—

She took refuge in her heart's conviction that he was safe, if sundered from her. He had been whole and strong and himself within the web.

Wherever he was, the enemy did not have him. She had to believe that, or she would lose whatever courage she had left.

"Riquier!"

Gereint's heart felt as if it were being rent from his body. When the web itself began to tear, he struck back blindly, with all his force.

The enemy recoiled. The web snapped shut upon itself. Gereint dropped like a poled ox.

For once when his magic had run free of his control, he held to consciousness. His mind was perfectly clear.

Riquier was dead. Averil was—Averil was—

"No," he said aloud. "No. I'd be dead, too."

He dragged himself to his feet. He had been performing his assigned duty: tending horses as always. Mauritius' destrier, in whose stall he had fallen over, stood warily against the wall. The big dark eye rolled as Gereint fumbled at the gate's latch.

The Rose was not destroyed. Not this time. But Knights were dead. A Squire was dead, destroyed for a secret he had not shared. That should have been Gereint's death, his torment. Because he knew—not everything. But enough to be dangerous.

He knew where the Serpent was, and who kept its prison.

"I should have kept it," he said. "I should have—"

Mauritius silenced him with a hand over his mouth. The Knight looked as haggard as Gereint felt, eyes like bruises in his ravaged face. "They have her," said the Knight. "They have the queen."

Gereint bit his tongue until it bled.

Mauritius said it for him. "We should have listened to you. Now we all pay."

"She won't break," Gereint said. "She won't tell them what she has."

"They may already know." Mauritius seemed undismayed, though if he was right, it was over; there was no hope. "Come with me."

Gereint did not move. "I'm riding out. Today. There's no time to waste."

"Haste will drive you to your death," Mauritius said.

"Come, messire. We'll have our grand rescue yet. For now—patience. Follow."

Gereint's jaw tightened. He did not want to see the sense in Mauritius' words—but damn the man, he was right. This was war. If he rode out to battle, he had to be prepared.

11

MAURITIUS LED GEREINT to the solar of the chapter house. Bernardin sat in one of the tall carved chairs—one of the few times Gereint had seen the Lord Protector off his feet and away from guardroom or practice court since the Ladies' magic snatched him out of Gemigny.

Ademar was with the Knight, playing the servant with wine and a basket of cakes. The guest who sat opposite Bernardin brought Gereint up short and nearly sent him at the gallop back to the stables.

Mauritius barred the door with more than his body. Gereint had no choice but to face the Lady from the chapel: the one who was neither young nor old, who had sat beside the eldest. She had seemed kind, he granted her. But she was what she was.

"This, messire," said Bernardin, "is the Lady Darienne. She has somewhat to say to you."

Gereint stood stiffly. He could not bring himself to bow. "Lady," he said, tight-lipped.

Her smile was faint but warm, and her eyes were warmer

still, with sympathy in them that he did not want or need to see. "Messire, I understand your grief, and somewhat of your anger. You were snatched away from a great charge. And yet, messire, if you had not been, you would be dead or worse, and she would be no better served."

Gereint's hands knotted into fists. The roar and surge of magic that would have blasted her, he held in check. She would never know how close she had come to dissolution. Even a year ago, there would have been no hope for her.

He could take no pride in his accomplishment. He marshaled his words instead, and spoke them as calmly as he might. "Lady, with all respect, you do not even begin to know what you have done. Only my lady knows, and her we may have lost."

"Those are strong words, messire," Bernardin said. "You will do well to—"

"My lord," Gereint said, "we've all kept secrets or kept silence, and for that I beg your pardon. Maybe it's mad of me to say anything now; you're all so blind, so locked into the world as you've been raised to see it. As for you, Lady, I don't know or trust you, and I probably should never say these things where you can hear. But do you know, I no longer care."

"Messire—" Bernardin began.

It was Mauritius, to Gereint's astonishment, who said, "No, my lord. Listen."

The Lady was listening already, intently. Gereint almost lost his nerve. Long speeches and spates of words were not his way; he kept himself to himself, and said as little as he could manage, mostly. But that had to stop now.

"My lords," he said. "Lady. The spell snared me because it was meant to. It was badly done and most ill-timed. It sundered my lady from her greatest strength. Longinus and Melusine, Lady. That is what we are. We are two who were meant to be one—just as they were."

"That is a legend," Darienne said.

"It is real," said Gereint. "Look at me, Lady. Really look. Don't try to turn it into something familiar. Just see."

It was one of the harder things he had done in his life, to stand there, open, with his defenses armed but laid aside. Her touch no doubt was as delicate as she knew how to make it, but it felt like the rake of dragons' claws.

She did not linger long. She drew back with a long sigh. Her face was pale; her eyes fixed on him as if they could not let go. "Child," she said, "do you know who you are? What you are?"

"I've begun to," he said. "Now, Lady, do you understand? Do you see what she has, and why I should never have been taken from her?"

"I understand," she said. "We did worse even than we knew."

"There can't be secrets," Gereint said, "not any more, nor intrigue between the Isle and the Rose. There can't be mistrust. We have to fight together, or we'll fall."

"Some secrets should never come to light," said Darienne.

"We'd best pray they don't," he said, "and do our utmost to keep them from it."

"Difficult," she said, "with the most terrible of them all in the enemy's hands."

"Only if he knows what he has. She won't betray it, Lady. Pray the good God we get her back before it betrays itself." Gereint lifted his eyes from the Lady to the Knights. "May I go?"

Mauritius was much as always. Bernardin looked as if he had taken a blow to the gut. Blindness was a bitter affliction, but its cure could be even worse.

Gereint understood a little of how they felt. Averil had suffered enough from it, torn between all she had thought she knew, and all she had come to know and see. It was a terrible and wrenching thing.

He had never been raised to distinguish between kinds or degrees of magic. For his mother, they had all been the same: lies and deception. She had almost destroyed him in her hatred of it, but in the end she had done him a great service. No barriers lay between Gereint and his powers. All that they were, whatever they were, it was all the same to him.

"My lord," he said to Bernardin, "every moment we delay, we slide closer to the edge. I'll ask you one last time. May I go?"

"Both of us will go," Mauritius said, "but first, we must be certain of the way. I doubt they'll keep her in Gemigny."

"They will not," said Bernardin. "If they have her, they'll be wanting not only what she has but what she is: what makes her queen. They will bring her to the kingdom's heart, and through her, take its soul."

Gereint shook his head. "Messire, that may be true. I'm only a Squire, and a poorly educated one at that. But I think that what they want is even simpler. They want to wake the Serpent. Either they know she carries the Mystery, or they suspect she knows where it is. Either way, I have to find her before they break her. I have to stop them." He drew a shuddering breath. "Please, before God. We're squandering time."

He was beginning to send off sparks. Darienne passed her hand over him, smoothing him down like a ruffled cat.

He stared at her. She was strong, to suffer so many shocks and still be standing. It seemed she had the measure of him—or thought she did. "There is more even than that, yes?" she said.

He started to shake his head, but then he paused. A fragment of memory seized and held him fast. He had seen it in the web, slipping by almost too swift to catch. "The chapel," he said, "in Caermor in Prydain. The first Knights. And . . ." It had been easy to say her name before, but now, somehow, it was almost impossibly difficult. "Melusine. They guard her in death as in life. And they guard another thing, a perilous thing. The key."

Darienne had gone very still. "How did you know of that?"

"My father told me," Gereint said.

"Your—" She stopped herself.

"My father is the Myrddin of Prydain," Gereint said.

Bernardin's brows had risen. Mauritius nodded. He knew already: he had eyes, after all.

"And she?" asked Darienne. "She knows?"

"She was with us," Gereint said. "We all saw."

Already Gereint knew this Lady was not one to give way to despair, but this last revelation weighed her down visibly.

She drew herself up with a clear effort of will. "So then. We've not seen the end yet, or none of us would be here. We can be sure the enemy knows of the Mysteries—the king took the lesser two when the Rose fell. Now, whether he knows it or not, the king's sorcerer has the great one. But the key . . . that is the greatest secret of all."

"And yet you know it," said Gereint. "Are you one of the nine Ladies, then? Or an ageless sorcerer?"

"I am one of nine," Darienne said. "My foremother was Madeleine."

Gereint had to bow to that. Madeleine had taken the children of Melusine the Betrayer and raised them as her own, protecting them against the long lie that was their mother's treason. One of those children had been Averil's forefather.

Strange and beyond strange to think of these high folk as kin. But Gereint was a Paladin's child, too—nearer to the source than any of them. His father was the youngest of all, the one who was neither human nor mortal, Peredur the Beloved.

That secret he was not about to tell. The rest had been hard enough. He could stand to be a great mage's son; he was a mage himself. He could not, just then, face the stares and incredulity if he told the whole truth.

Maybe the Lady already knew. Her eyes on him were very sharp. But she said nothing except, "As you say, time is flying. I think I know where they may go, and how we may come there before them. Will you let me guide you?"

Gereint had his doubts that they could move more

swiftly than the Serpent's servants. They had tarried too long already, squabbling over trifles. But even if they came late, at least they would have tried.

He bent his head to her. "Do as you will, Lady."

IT BEGAN WITH magery, with scrying and foreseeing. Gereint was not asked to share in it. His task was to rest and be patient—grueling ordeals both.

He finished tending the horses as he had been doing when Riquier died. Then he sought out one of the practice courts, but there was no one to trade blows with him. He took refuge behind the kitchens instead, chopping wood for the fires until every log was cut and there was nothing left to render into kindling.

His arms ached; his body ran with sweat despite the cold. He buried the axe in the block, all the way to the haft, and dropped down beside it.

He had no tears for Riquier. Someday he would. Now he had only a deep and abiding anger.

For Averil he did not know what he had. Fear. Desperation. A rending sense of loss, of emptiness where her presence should have been.

He squeezed his eyes shut. Memory—he had that. The warmth of her hand in his. The light in her eyes when she looked at him. The clean uncomplicated scent of her; the taste of her lips when once, and only once in the waking world though often enough in dream, he had had the temerity to steal a kiss.

That was as vivid a memory as he could have wished for.

She tasted like honey, and a little like wine. Her breath mingled with his. Her voice was hardly more than a whisper. "Gold," she said. "Golden Wood. Remember."

He started out of his half-dream. She had been so real, so near—her kiss still burned.

Too late he snatched at the rags of the dream. It was gone, and Averil with it. But her words lingered in his mind. He spoke them aloud. "Golden Wood."

He had heard those words before. When he was wider awake, he would remember where, and what they meant. In this moment, he only knew that she had reached through the walls of sorcery, and for an instant, she had touched him.

He scrambled to his feet. It was a straw for the grasping, as frail and insubstantial as such a thing could be. But it was better than nothing at all.

12

AVERIL'S SOUL SPUN dizzily back into her body. She had been mad to try what she had; she could not even be sure she had succeeded. But she held to the rags of a dream, the fading memory of a kiss. That had been Gereint—it had. She had found him even with her magic taken away, and even through the walls that the sorcerer had raised.

She had no magic left now; nothing to conjure with. She clung to the saddle of the docile mare she had been given when she refused, with barely constrained violence, to be packed away in a carriage with Mathilde. One of Gamelin's blank-eyed guards held the rein as he had since she was taken out of Gemigny.

They were all around her, bodies with breath but no souls, marching in eerie unison according to the will of their master. They felt no pain, knew neither heat nor cold. When they ate as bodies must, they took whatever they were given.

They were eating the kingdom alive, both to nourish

themselves and to add to their numbers. It was madness—
Serpent madness, raising armies first to conquer the kingdom, then to feed the great beast when it woke from its
long sleep.

There was a monstrous economy in it, a tidy practicality
worthy of a village housewife. It made Averil's stomach heave.

So many souls lost. So many sons and brothers and
lovers worse than dead. There was no way to bring their
souls back—the Knights said so, and the mages of every order she had been able to ask. This darkest of dark magics,
once made, could not be unmade.

Maybe the wild magic could unmake it. Gereint would
know—or Peredur. Averil might know herself, somewhere
down deep, where she lacked the courage to go.

She had nothing to do now except ride and endure and
plumb the depths of herself. It pleased her enemy to let her
keep only one of all her magics, to know what he did and
when and how, and to be utterly helpless to touch or
change what she saw.

She refused to let him conquer her with rage or frustra-
tion. She counted ranks in the army, and listened and reckoned and committed every moment to memory, in hope,
however vain, that she might find a way to warn her Knights.

Two thousand bodies without souls rode as her escort,
and ten and twenty times that number advanced on other
roads toward Lutèce, and the armies gathered there behind
walls of sorcery. They would reveal themselves soon, when
the Rose had spread itself vanishingly thin, and such forces
as it could muster were stolen away, soul-taken and en-
spelled and bound to the sorcerer's will.

The order was fighting hard. Sometimes it won a victory, and a hundred or five hundred or a thousand men died in the body as well as in the soul. But always there were more, and once there was a cry of triumph as a brother of the Rose fell. Then Averil mourned, but her eyes and mind refused to dim or weaken. The more her enemy strove to break her, the stronger she determined to be.

He rode behind her in a large and thickly curtained carriage, much like the one to which she had objected so strenuously. Wagons followed, heavy laden with she knew not what. But she could guess.

Gold and treasure, certainly. Instruments of sorcery. One, a massive box on wheels, reeked of magic; when she was led past it on her way from Gemigny, she had felt the heat radiating from it, and heard the hissing inside. It was full of serpents.

They had begun in a bitter-bright morning, and ridden through to darkness; camped under stars, then gone forth when the light returned. Averil counted days as she counted armies, with a kind of fierce despair—the armies because they were too many, and the days because they were too few. This journey should be taking far longer, and giving her people far more time to raise defenses.

The roads they took were seldom mortal roads. She recognized the light of other worlds, though the land seemed unchanged, locked deep in winter's barrenness. They passed no towns or villages; those did not matter now, except for Lutèce. No wildfolk found them, and no magic moved here but what surrounded their riding.

Prince Esteban had ridden out of Gemigny with the

army, but all too soon he left it. Alone and strong and skilled in magic, unencumbered by the mass of soulless bodies, he ventured even swifter ways than these, to nurture his conspiracies and prepare the way for his ally's invasion.

The sorcerer's spells were not set to bind him; he was free of all roads. He could travel five days' journey in an hour, there and back again, and mock them all with the ease of his passing.

He was waiting for them at a crossroad as the sun touched the zenith, surrounded by men in Morescan armor, chased with silver or copper and crowned with crimson plumes. All of those were safely and entirely mortal, and none too happy to be so close to so many of the soulless.

Their lord, whose armor was chased with gold and whose horse wore trappings of crimson silk, looked ready to ride in parade through the royal city. And so it seemed he had been doing, as he fell into the column beside Gamelin's carriage. "No change as yet in the city," he said. "The Rose dissipates its strength in hunting down our scattered companies, and remains as blind as ever to the army that marches under your spell. I heard a man or two suggest that our wards must conceal an ambush, but the commanders show no sign of listening to them."

"Good," said Gamelin. "You strengthened the workings?"

"As much as I might," Esteban said. "There are undercurrents, I grant you, but none that troubles me. We caught a mage spying as we rode through Lutèce: a rustic sort of fellow, hawking herbs and simples on a corner. He had the stink of the Rose on him. I cast a glamour over him. He'll tell his masters nothing but that the ambassador from Moresca went to market and bought a napkinful of venison pasties and a very pretty pair of dueling blades."

Gamelin hissed with impatience. "Never mind that. We've no need to hear the life's tale of every fool you happen upon. The rest is done?"

"As much as it may be," said Esteban.

"There's nothing more to do, then," Gamelin said. "Now go back where you belong. It was unwise of you to walk that road with so many, and in broad daylight. Fools and blind the Rose may be, but even they can smell a working of that magnitude, if it's done beneath their noses."

"The Rose knows nothing," Esteban said. "I took every precaution. Their spy never saw us go; no one else was looking—I made sure of that. I'll ride with you, messire, since as you say, the rest is done. It only needs your coming to be complete."

Gamelin had more to say, but Esteban bowed with courtesy that was the most exquisite insolence, and turned his back on him.

Averil had no desire to play the games of courts, here or anywhere. When that glittering figure halted beside her, she stared through him. It was not as easy as she wanted it to be. He was a lovely thing, and a brave sight, too.

"Lady," he said. There was no insolence in that, apart from what was always in him. His bow seemed honest in its respect, and in its outrage at her condition. "Why are you riding in the cold? Could they not be troubled to spare you a carriage?"

"I don't want one," Averil said. "I like the cold."

"Ah," he said, only slightly nonplussed. "I should have known. Still, they could have mounted you more suitably, and dressed you more warmly."

"I'm warm enough," she said.

"Even so," he said, sweeping his mantle of crimson silk and ermine from his shoulders and wrapping it around her. The mare barely flicked an ear. His stallion snorted and danced; he held it in place with the sheer elegance of his seat, hardly touching the rein.

Averil succumbed for a dangerous instant to that heavenly and luxurious warmth. Then she let it slither to the ground. "I am warm enough," she repeated.

Esteban winced as Gamelin's soldiers trampled his beautiful and costly cloak into the mud of the road, but he seemed immune to anger. "I understand, lady. You believe yourself betrayed."

"I know I am."

"You're right to be angry," he said. "This is not the world you were raised for. But think, lady. Might it not, in the end, be better?"

"We've indulged in that disputation before," she said. "I made my choice. Was it not clear?"

"It was clear," he said. "But that, lady, was when you had a choice."

His tone was mild, his expression amiable, but his words had an edge of steel.

The malaise that had gripped Averil was gone. This was war. "So," she said. "I'm to be seized and married by force."

"If necessary," he said. He managed to sound as if he regretted the force, if not the necessity.

"You think I'd assent to it now, after all that's passed?"

He shrugged, the lift of a shoulder. "You pride yourself in your practicality. Be practical, then, and consider. We hold you captive. Our army outnumbers any that your people can muster. You can, if you act wisely, save your people, and even your allies of the Rose. Those are dear to you, I know."

"We've not lost this war yet," she said.

"Assent to this and there will be no war at all."

"What will there be? Armies of soulless soldiers, and sorcerers in command of every town? If I accept you, am I your queen or your puppet?"

"Lady, if the queen were one of us, she would rule us all."

"Will you swear to that?"

"With all my heart, lady," said Esteban.

Averil frowned at the mare's mane. She trusted this man not at all, nor reckoned his oath worth the breath he took to swear it. And yet there was some faint seduction in the thought of taking the throne in whatever way she could, and doing what good she might once she was queen.

She slid a glance at the prince. By law Averil must marry. Her rank and position allowed her to choose the man, but she was far from the first to lose that right of choice. Songs and tales were full of such things.

Averil meant her life to be more than a verse in an old ballad. If they sang of her, they would sing that she escaped her captors and won the war and restored the kingdom to its old glory.

Escape was a distant unlikelihood at the moment. With an army all around her, her magic cut off from her, and no friend or ally at her back, she could well say that she was in poor straits.

She had not given up yet. The road looked mortal enough, winding through winter-fallow fields and bits of woodland, but there was no mistaking that slight blurring of the edges. It was shortening itself all but invisibly, taking a straighter way than an earthly road could do.

Averil had taken for granted that this was another of Gamelin's sorceries, but as she examined the working more closely, she marked the signs of a different magic. There was no mistaking the faint but distinct flavor of the Isle. Mathilde in her carriage was doing more than lie on cushions and dream the long hours away.

EVEN WITH MATHILDE's working to shorten the way, by evening they were still on the road. The army's dead weight dragged at its masters' magic—enough almost to give Averil hope.

The ranks of the soulless camped in a wide open field. The high ones and their prisoner lodged in the abbey to which the field belonged.

As with the army, the Church had suffered sorely from Gamelin's sorceries. The abbey was nearly empty of monks; the abbot bowed before Gamelin, all but speechless with terror. His guesthouse had an air of disuse, but it was clean, and warm once Mathilde's maids built up the fire in the hearth.

Averil had no appetite for the frugal feast that the abbot

offered. She ate to keep her body alive, and excused herself from his table as soon as she might.

Guards followed her back to the guesthouse; two of Mathilde's maids walked with her. There were eyes on her always.

She kept her head down and let her shoulders droop, as if she had given up hope of escape. She let the maids undress her, as docile as a captive should be, and lay on the bed to which they led her, farthest from either door or window. It was warm at least in that corner, and sleep, like bread and hard cheese and pickled onions, was a useful thing.

In sleep she could dream. Maybe she would dream of Gereint. And maybe he would dream of her.

13

GEMIGNY WAS EMPTY. One of the Lord Protector's companies, ranging far afield, had won through the sorcerer's fog and sent a spy to find the queen. He came back almost intact, with word that the lady and her guests had gone. They were nowhere to be found on any of the roads, by magic or by mortal eyes.

The earth knew where they were. One only had to know how, and what, to ask. Gereint walked the streets of Lutèce in the days after Riquier died, tracing the lines of old tracks now paved over but still perceptible beneath.

He was still in the city, not because he had given up the hunt, but because his heart kept telling him this was where she would come. The Knights and their allies searched the whole of Lys for some sign of her. He had a memory and a dream, and a conviction that if he only knew how to open his eyes, he would find her.

Once he woke fully, he remembered the Golden Wood— as he should. Averil herself had told him of it. It was a forest of beeches and birches west of the city, an old garden of kings. There was a hunting lodge in it, and herds of deer and boar, and a lake rich with waterfowl. Beneath it, there were mysteries.

Serpent mages had taken Averil there once already, and so appalled her that she had fled into exile in Prydain rather than give way to their temptations. It seemed rather too obvious that they would try the same tactic again. Surely they would find another hiding place, or snatch her out of Lys altogether.

His elders and betters were searching everywhere beyond the orbit of Lutèce, all the way to the far side of the world. A Knight and a pair of Squires had even set out for the Isle.

Here in the city, Bernardin and Mauritius went on mustering forces both martial and magical. Some they flung against any enemy they seemed able to find—a diversion from that other and stronger force with which they hoped to ambush the sorcerer's ambush.

They believed they had found a weakness in his plan: as strong as his wall of nothingness might be, it had boundaries, and the Knights had the power to trace them. Within them, the Knights were certain, was all of the army that the king had raised, that had not drowned in the sea.

They had no time to count it, to reckon the tally of each town and village and find those who kept their souls and those who had vanished without a trace. But from the numbers that they had found, they could hazard a guess.

It was a war of shadows. Gereint was glad to be a lowly Squire and not a Knight Commander, charged with defending a broken realm against an intangible enemy.

As a lowly Squire, too weak in arms to ride out on forays

and too closely bound to the queen to let out of his elders' reach, he had little to do but look after the horses and carry on with his weapons practice. When he was done with those, they had no objection to his wandering the city—as long as he did not try to pass the outer walls.

The currents of magic in this place were strong and deep and very old. He had not yet followed them to the Wood; that would need an escape of sorts, and more surety than he yet had. He could not feel that she was there, not in the earth, and not in his heart.

But she would be. Therefore he waited and strove for patience, and tried not to go wild over where she must be or what her captors must be doing to her. They would not destroy her, not quite. They needed her alive, to be their puppet.

The third day after the Ladies snatched him away from Gemigny, Gereint paused in one of the many markets of Lutèce. In winter it was the province of butchers and bakers and cheesemongers, raising among them such a fragrance that even as sick at heart as he was, he stopped and stood and breathed deep.

It was magic of a sort, solid and earthbound and in its own way wonderful. He paid a penny for a warm loaf split and filled with roast pig and herbed cheese, and ate it in the street. People jostled past him, occasionally taken aback by his size, but mostly intent on their own preoccupations.

"Ademar," he said to the air, "no need to lurk and spy. Come out and keep me company."

The Novice emerged from concealment in the alley beside the baker's shop. He was, as always, insouciant. "Seeing through wards again, are you?"

"Always," said Gereint. He divided the remains of the loaf in two and handed half to Ademar. While the Novice devoured it, Gereint sank back into himself, letting words drain away in the purity of the senses.

Powers moved above and below. Far and deep, he sensed a familiar presence, old and cold and sated with its feast of ships and sailors and one unlamented king.

The king's sorcerer had learned that lesson at least: wherever he had gone, it was not to the deeps of the earth. Nor would he brave the air, where the wild magic grew stronger with each sunrise.

Even here in the heart of Lys, Gereint could feel it rising. Wildfolk had not come here in force, not yet, but they were gathering along the edges of this rigidly ordered world.

Serpent magic had opened a door. As it crept through the ordered spaces of the kingdom, breaking them apart and crumbling them into ruin, all the small wild things had room to move and grow.

Wild magic had never ruled, or tried to. It was what it was. When other magics failed, it was still there, like the breath in a living body.

Magic of the orders had driven it out, but it breathed still beneath, woven through the fabric of all that was. It slept in the earth; it drifted on the wind.

It knew where Averil was. Everything was contained in it—Gereint, too, with his magic that had never yielded to any order.

Since he came to the Rose, he had learned one kind of magic, the magic that lived in the crystalline structures of glass. The rest had grown on its own, sometimes wild, sometimes reluctantly and imperfectly tamed. The part that he shared with Averil had shape and substance, but there was always an undertone of guilt and secrecy— because she was royal and he was anything but that, and what they had was like nothing else that they or anyone near them knew.

He had to let it all go. No more constraint. No more fear of what might happen.

"You look as if you swallowed the sun."

Ademar's voice brought Gereint back into the lesser world. The Novice did not stoop to awe, but his eyes were a little wide. "What were you doing? What working was that?"

"I don't think it has a name," Gereint said.

"Did you find her?"

Ademar always went straight to the point. Gereint shook his head. "I think I know how to look for her, but I don't know how long it will take. Will you help?"

"If I can," said Ademar. "I don't really know what you were doing. It's not any magic I've seen before."

"My magic mostly isn't," Gereint said. "There's little enough to do. Just keep spying on me, and stop me if the magic starts to swallow me whole."

"I can do that," said Ademar. "I think."

"Good man." Gereint began to walk where his feet led him. As he went, a skein of wildfolk trailed behind him, silent and all but transparent. He might not have known they were there at all, if his magic had not been at fever pitch.

They were watching as Ademar was. What they would do, whether they could or would protect him, he did not know. Still, their presence comforted him. It was a great thing for them to brave the anguish of ordered magic, and to appear, even in such tenuous form, within the walls of Lutèce.

GEREINT'S FEET LED him in a great spiral, sunwise through the streets of the city. At the heart of the spiral he found himself in front of the cathedral of the Holy Mother.

He staggered and nearly went down. He had been on the Field of the Binding where the Young God died and the Serpent was bound. He had walked in the Wildlands and spoken to the Mother of gods. He had persuaded the cold-drake of Prydain to destroy the sorcerers who had raised it. He was no stranger to great upwellings of magic.

The center of it all was here. All roads led to this place; all magical tracks began and ended where Gereint stood.

He almost fell again, as understanding struck him. The Serpent had not been bound on the battlefield. It had been bound here. The city, the cathedral, had grown up where the magic was strongest, driving it deep and burying it in oblivion.

Peredur must know. The rest had forgotten, as they had taught themselves to forget the truth of Melusine.

The truth was broken like a pane of colored glass, divided in shards and set in lead and made into an image that bore only a faint resemblance to its original shape. Maybe it was simpler so; maybe it suited the purpose of the mage who wrought the glass, or the Church in whose shrine it hung.

Gereint was in shards, too, with Averil lost and his father found and the shadow of war hanging over them all. The magic in this place fed him strength that might save him—or might be the end of him. He was too strong for his skill as it was. Without Averil, he had little hope of controlling that strength.

He had no choice but to learn, even though there was no time. He had a teacher, if he would ask—and if Peredur would teach.

If he could find Peredur. The mage was gone again. Alone of all who endured under the sorcerer's shadow, he came and went at will, without any sense or reason that Gereint had been able to decipher.

That need not matter. Gereint addressed him as if he had been standing in the square, in every confidence that wherever he was, he could hear. "I need you. Come, please. Help."

The answer was less a word than a murmur in the heart. *Patience.*

"There's no time left for that," Gereint said. "Come and help."

In due time. Wait. Be patient.

Gereint lashed him with barely bridled temper, but there was nothing left to be blasted into shards. Peredur was gone, sunk back into the well of magic.

The earth rocked gently underfoot, then steadied. Gereint let his anger drain away.

He breathed deep once and then again. He had come to the Rose for discipline. He could hardly fault Peredur for reminding him of that.

He left a part of himself in the well, like a small and supple child of the wild magic, darting lizard-quick from shadow to shadow. If Averil touched it, or if anyone close to her came near it, he would know.

It was a small thing and might be useless, but it cost him little. It was a comfort of sorts: it made him feel as if, however feebly, he was at least trying to do something.

14

PRYDAIN'S QUEEN KNELT in a pool of light, the magic of sunlight through jeweled glass poured out on her chapel floor. To her maids and servants who watched, she seemed to be praying.

She was Lady as well as queen, and in the enchantment of living light, she spoke to those of her sisters who ruled both openly and in secret through the kingdoms of the world. They were Nine, and they matched the Nine who guarded the fastness of the Isle.

"Soon now," said one in Lys, and one in Moresca, and one far to the east. Their voices sang together like the descant of a hymn.

That from the east rose above the rest, an echo of temple bells, with a shimmer behind it of golden skin and long dark eyes. "The wheel of the ages has turned. Those who were forgotten have come again. What they bring with them . . ."

"Could we have stopped it?" The wind of the north was in that voice, the cold of snow and the emptiness of vast fields of ice. She was old, that Lady, and wise, and very strong. "Should we wish to?"

"Change is deadly," said the Lady in Moresca. "The world we made will be forever changed. Dare we risk that?"

"I think we must," said the Lady in Lys.

The gathering trembled. Queen Eiluned swayed on her knees, buffeted by the storm of magic that rose through the aether.

"You," said she of the east, turning the fire of her focus on Eiluned. "You keep the key. Is that wise? Is it time to destroy it?"

"We should have destroyed it long ago," said the Lady in Moresca. "We were fools to let it remain in the world."

"There was no letting in that," Eiluned said. "The wards that protect it are as strong as those that guard the Mystery."

"Then I advise we break them," the Morescan said. "Our enemy has the Mystery. If he takes possession of the key as well—"

"The key is safe," said Eiluned, sharp as a door shutting.

She left the gathering then, calmly as she thought, until she realized she was shaking. Their doubt was wise, but it was also an insult. One would have thought they did not trust her.

Trust was a rare commodity in this world. One acolyte of the Isle in Lys was already lost, turned traitor to them all. God and His holy Mother knew how many more there were.

Eiluned's charge lay in a crypt in her own city, surrounded by magics both ancient and strong. The tomb in which it rested belonged to Melusine herself; her power was still in it, and the power of the Knights who had protected her in life and defended her in death.

Eiluned rose stiffly. The floor was cold, but never as cold

as her heart. She called for her most trusted servant and
bade him come to her in a place somewhat warmer and less
public than the royal chapel.

PRINCE GORONWY DID not make a habit of spying on his
aunt, but in winter especially, when rain and sleet and biting winds kept even the hardiest within doors, there was
little to do but lurk and gossip and indulge in intrigue.
Goronwy, the old king's son, who should have been king,
was the center of many of those intrigues. He did take pleasure in them, but he liked to be alone, too, with his thoughts
and his magic.

There was a great deal of magic to learn, these days, but
all of it had to be learned in secret. It was not a kind of
magic that the orders would approve of.

On that particular day, Goronwy had been practicing a
new art of listening and remembering. One performed it in
solitude if one could, with a dark glass and a vial of a most
peculiar and versatile potion. Goronwy found it more interesting to imbibe a drop of the potion and go walking
through palace or city and see what found him.

The beauty of the spell was that if one incanted it just so,
it rendered one as transparent as glass. In strong enough
light, a keen eye could see an outline of a man, but in the
light of lamps or candles that illuminated most rooms in
the palace, he was invisible.

He had been a shimmer in the corner of his aunt's
chapel, unseen and unremarked. Most of what passed there,
he had not been able to make sense of, but he knew there
were more presences within those walls than the eye could

see. Now and then he glimpsed something in the swirl of
light around the queen: a face, a form; he caught a word or
two, hardly enough to count as a fragment, but it intrigued
him.

After she had summoned her best-beloved spy to the solar, Goronwy hastened ahead, moving so quickly he almost
outran the spell. But he kept a grip on it, and no one saw
him flitting along the edges of courts and passages.

In the solar he settled in a corner near the fire, but not
so close that its light betrayed him. He had, on a previous
venture, seen to it that there was a stool there, which none
of the servants had since ventured to remove.

He was growing restless when the queen arrived at last,
followed by her friend and frequent confidant, the lord Dylan Fawr.

Goronwy loathed Dylan Fawr. Not only was the man half
a woman, with his entourage of mincing boys; he was half a
Knight, too, so close a friend to the Rose that some said he
must have been one of their acolytes when he was younger.
But he had never risen to such a height, as a man or as a
mage.

Eiluned seldom stood on ceremony when she was, as she
thought, alone. She had dismissed her maids and ordered
the guards to stand outside. That was so rare a thing that
Goronwy hugged himself in silent glee. Oh, these were secrets indeed—and he would hear them, he the forgotten
one, the disregarded, whom she barely acknowledged even
when she could see him.

Dylan Fawr bowed as he entered, and accepted a cup of
wine from the royal hand. He sipped it daintily, murmuring

of nothing, as if even here he could not forsake his habit of toadying to his betters.

Eiluned cut him short. "My friend, I have a thing to ask of you. If it's excessive, do say so; this is nothing I can force on you."

"I am always at your service, Lady," he said.

"I don't ask for service in this," she said, but with no sign of impatience. "It must be freely given."

He paused. His face changed; it lost some of its foolishness and much of its softness. He looked almost like a man then, and almost formidable. "Tell me, Lady," he said.

Goronwy held his breath. Eiluned took an endless while to gather her words together. "In the city," she said, "there is a place which needs the strongest but also the subtlest defense. It needs a mage and a knight, and one familiar with serpent magic. Above all, it needs a defender whom I can trust beyond death."

Dylan Fawr held steady. All vestige of subservience was gone. He met his queen's stare. "May you tell me what I guard?"

"The key to the world's end," she answered. "You will know it when you see it. I can give you no mages, no guards—there is none whom I trust."

"You can trust the Rose," he said.

"Not in this."

He looked as if he might object, but she was, after all, the queen. "Very well, Lady. I will do what I may."

"Do it well," she said, "and you save us all."

She left the alternative unspoken. Dylan Fawr bowed one

last time and kissed her hand, then left so quickly that
Goronwy barely slipped through the door before it closed.

GORONWY'S HEART BEAT hard. This was not the first daring
thing he had done, but in his bones he knew it was the most
important.

He should have been given this task. *He* should have been
the queen's champion. He was as royal as she.

But, he thought as he ghosted in Dylan Fawr's wake, if he
was royal, and if the throne in fact belonged to him, he was
much too valuable to risk. She must know that. She trusted
him. She would not waste his life or soul, that was all.

If he felt a flicker of remorse, it was no more than that. He
would never be king unless he reached out to take the prize.
Even his teachers had told him as much. They could not give
him the throne. He had to win it for himself.

This would give it to him. Whatever key Dylan Fawr was to
guard with his life and soul, it must be a mighty and terrible
thing. If Goronwy had it, who knew what powers he could
gain?

It was a long hunt. Dylan Fawr withdrew to his own house
first, where the latest of his succession of lovers hacked
doggedly at the pells—as if anyone needed a sword that heavy
in this age of the world. The boy must do it for the muscles it
gave him: he was a brawny creature, with a beard so strong it
shadowed his jaw within moments of his shaving it.

Goronwy had no desire to loiter about while they indulged
in dalliance, but luck was with him. "My love," said Dylan
Fawr, "it's time. The battle has begun."

Young Baron Fourchard came to the alert like a hound on a keen scent. He looked from side to side as if he expected to find an army in the courtyard, and relaxed only slightly when Dylan Fawr said, "Not that kind of battle. Not yet. Fetch your cloak and follow."

Fourchard fetched his cloak and kept his sword. He loomed formidably behind his shorter, slighter lover. Goronwy, shorter still and happily invisible, glided in their mingled shadow.

They took a winding path through a city notorious for its interlocking circles and spirals. Goronwy stopped trying to remember each twist and turn. He marked their movement instead by the tower of the cathedral and the turnings of the river.

They circled halfway round the tower and past the White Quay with its walls of marble from Romagna, then turned toward the old city. It was long outgrown now, its streets too narrow and its houses too low and small; it was mostly the haunt of the poor and the inhuman and the hopelessly unfashionable. Goronwy went there as seldom as he could.

Dylan Fawr and his hulking escort made their way unerringly to the center of it. A mean little hovel of a church stood there, so old it barely had a tower.

If Goronwy had to hide a treasure that no one should ever find, he would hide it in such a place as this. He tracked his quarry into the dim and musty nave, and then down to a surprisingly capacious crypt.

He wavered at the top of the stair. All at once, his courage abandoned him. He was invisible, he was safe—but he had a sudden and inexplicable horror of whatever lay below.

The place stank of long-dead roses and something else, something deeper and stronger and older. It was a cold smell; a dead smell, he would have said, and yet there was life in it.

It was faint under the reek of roses, but still it called to him. Shuddering, gasping with terror, he tensed to turn and run—but when he moved, it was to stumble down the steep, narrow stair.

TWELVE TOMBS AND one lay in that place, each with its stone effigy of an antique knight—except for the last, the farthest from the stair. Nothing lay on that stone; no name was carved there.

Dylan Fawr and his looming shadow stood in front of it. Goronwy felt the prickle of magic in his skin. Slow light grew around the tomb.

It had an effigy after all: not a knight but a lady, lying as if asleep. The lines of her face were hauntingly familiar. On her breast, clasped in her hands as each of the knights clasped a sword, was a thing like a curved dagger, made not of metal but of what seemed like milky glass.

"The Serpent's tooth." Fourchard's whisper filled the chamber with hissing echoes. "So it's true. The rumor— the legend—it told the truth."

Dylan Fawr nodded. His shoulders bent as if beneath the weight of the world. "This is the key. If our enemies find it and the door that it opens, there's no hope for any of us."

"We'll guard it," Fourchard said. "Your magic, my sword— who can stand against us?"

Dylan Fawr laughed with a wry twist. "Who indeed? Who in the world is stronger than we?"

15

AVERIL'S DREAMS WERE dark, full of wind and rushing water. Voices babbled all around her, a madness of sound without sense.

She had lost her center. Her magic drifted far apart from the rest of her.

She could go mad. Or she could focus, narrowly and intensely, on the one bright thing in this endless night. It was minute, the merest pinprick, faint as the most distant star.

The earth shook. Mountains fell. But the star shone undimmed. She let the darkness go, until there was only light, and in that light . . .

"RELEASE THE SPELL."

She knew that voice. It went with a face, narrow and dark. He looked and sounded rather desperate.

"Let her go. You're killing her."

"That is not my spell," said one paler, older, with a slither of serpents about him. Him, too, she knew, to her sorrow. "I cast her into sleep, no more. This is another working, of which I know nothing."

"Undo it," said Esteban. "Undo it now."

"I cannot," said Gamelin.

"Try!"

Esteban's passion swept over her like a wash of flame. It neither burned nor troubled her. It was nothing to her.

She was losing the light, just as she understood that it was a beacon. Gereint had set it. If she could reach it, touch it, she would find her way back to him.

It was too far and she was too weak. That weakness was Gamelin's spell. She withered it with hate.

He recoiled. Gereint's beacon was lost, but she had her body's strength back again, a trickle at first but growing slowly.

The world took shape around her. The walls that rose above her were never those of the monastery in which she had fallen into sorcerous sleep. These were no work of hands, mortal or otherwise: they had grown in draperies and curtains of flowing stone, fantastic pillars and columns entwined with sinuous figures, and a floor that rippled like the floor of the sea. Subtle jewel-colors glowed in the light of lamps, catching the shimmer of a wide, deep pool.

She had been in this chamber before. It lay far beneath the earth; far above it, woven through with wards that concealed it from mages' senses, a royal hunting lodge sat in the heart of the Golden Wood.

She was half a day's journey from Lutèce and some fair portion of that below it, walled and warded with twice a thousand years of magic and memory. Whether the Serpent had dug this cavern or found it already shaped in the womb of the earth, the great beast had dwelt here. The power of its presence lingered.

It slept beyond the world's knowledge, imprisoned in a working of magic so great it had no sense of magic at all. She did her utmost to forget it now, in this of all places, even as it came just short of burning the tender skin of her breast.

Averil's captors had raised a pavilion near the pool and spread a soft bed for her, with hangings of silk and sendal, velvet and shimmering brocade.

She was too plainly dressed for such a bed, and some-what indifferently clean. But there was a remedy for that: a silver basin, steaming gently, wreathed in the scent of roses.

Perhaps they did not mean to be cruel. Averil doubted it. The water beckoned: her skin itched. She would remember the Knights, and think of hope.

She was back in the waking world now, after a fashion, and remarkably steady on her feet, all things considered. The hands that reached to undress her belonged to another of her captors' ironies: the Lady Mathilde, playing the servant. It would have been gratifying to cast her off with curses, but it was wiser and perhaps more disconcerting to Averil's captors to suffer the woman's touch.

Averil breathed deep of warmth and roses. The pendant slid between her breasts. Mathilde reached for it, to take it off with the rest.

Averil mustered a smile, a shake of the head, a slight shrug. Mathilde smiled in return, and arched a brow. "A lover's gift?"

Averil inclined her head. It had been—though he had not known what it was when he gave it.

"Very pretty," said Mathilde as Averil stepped into the basin.

Averil presented her back for washing: a small gesture, yet pointed. The hiss of Mathilde's breath told her that the dart had struck its target.

Good, thought Averil. The woman deserved no better.

Mathilde was skilled and her hands were gentle. Averil refused to be lulled into letting down her guard. Part of her could not believe that she was truly in danger, but the rest knew better.

Clean and warm and more richly dressed than she had been in some while, Averil turned without surprise to look into the face of the old king's sorcerer. He stood just outside the pavilion with Prince Esteban behind him like a guardsman, flanked by soulless soldiers.

Had they watched her bathe? Then she wished them joy of it.

She kept her chin up and her eyes steady. She would give them nothing, not even a word.

They did not ask for one. Two of the soldiers stepped into the pavilion, blank-eyed, expressionless. They caught and held her fast. The false priest reached for the chain that hung around her neck.

She stood helpless, reeling on the edge of despair. He knew what the pendant was—he must have known since his rape of the Knights' web. She was lost. There was no hope left.

The pendant burned no more fiercely than it had since she was taken, but as his fingers brushed it, he recoiled with a hiss. Her nose twitched at the stink of burning flesh.

He cradled his hand. His eyes were flat.

"So," said Esteban. He sounded rather satisfied. "It has defenses. I rather thought it might."

"It is bound to the one who guards it," Gamelin said, "and she to it. That complicates matters somewhat, but changes nothing."

Averil set her lips together. If they expected her to offer defiance, she would disappoint them.

It seemed they had no expectations. Gamelin left her without a word. Esteban nodded to Mathilde, and held her gaze until she retreated.

The sorcerer's soldiers followed her, though Averil had heard or sensed no command. As they ascended the long stair into the greater world, Averil wandered as if by chance to the wall that rimmed the pool.

Sunk deep in it was a great working, an image of the Serpent in its prison. The colors of it reflected those of the pendant she wore: red and gold, green and blue. She looked down on those sleeping coils, evading the unblinking golden eye—as if the image could see her, or the prisoner know what or who she was.

Esteban came to stand beside her. "It's fitting, don't you think? The queen of Lys guards the greatest of Mysteries. Did you know what it was when it came to you?"

He was perceptive. That could be a trap. Still, Averil answered him honestly. "It was a gift."

"From a lover."

"You were listening."

He shrugged infinitesimally. "It doesn't matter to me what you do or with whom, once the marriage is made. I only ask that if you produce children, those children be mine."

"That presumes I'll marry you," she said.

"Yes," said Esteban. "Clearly your lover is not suitable, or you'd have married him already. What is he? A Knight of the Rose? They're not celibate, except the handful that are priests. It seems foolish that they don't marry."

Averil happened to agree, but she would hardly say so to this man. "It's a tradition," she said.

"Certainly it serves our purpose," said Esteban. "I've persuaded our ally to delay the rite, in hopes that you'll come to it willingly. He won't wait long, now he's sure of what you carry; but we have at least the night."

Averil's back tightened. What little she had ever felt for him had vanished with her captivity. He was a comely thing, but she would no more embrace him than she would embrace a dark and gleaming serpent.

He reached with exquisite gentleness and touched her cheek. "I won't give you cause for regrets, lady. We'll be honest with one another. I can be loyal to you, and will, as a man is to his queen."

"And in return? What do you get, besides sons?"

"Queen's consort of Lys is no small office," he said.

"Even in the world you would make? Ranks and nations won't matter then, will they? We'll all be prey for the Serpent."

"The mortal world will still need ruling," said Esteban. "Who better for that than those who freed the Great One?"

"You think I'd ever do that?"

"I think you might be persuaded," he said. And as she

shook her head, set more firmly than ever against him, he smiled. "Give it time, lady. But tonight, rest a little. Set cares and sorrows aside. See what we might have together. Who knows? You might even learn to love me."

Not in this world, she thought.

He held out his hand. "Come."

She tensed to refuse, but his smile and the slant of his brow led her gaze toward the stair.

However beautiful this hall was, it was still a prison. If she could escape to the lodge above, she might have some hope of breaking free altogether.

It was a faint hope, but it was all she had. She let him take her hand. Though his touch was light, he made no effort to conceal his strength.

Not all strength was of the body. Averil embarked willingly enough on the long ascent.

16

ON THE MORNING of the dark of the year, six days after Riquier died, the sorcerer's fog lifted at last. Everywhere the defenders of Lutèce turned their eyes, an army of the soulless stood motionless, glittering darkly in the sun.

It was vast beyond counting. These could not only be the sons of Lys. The sorcerer, or the king who began the work before him, must have overrun the far side of the world and stripped it of its men, to bring so many to this field.

The roads and the river were closed off. The markets were empty. No pilgrims came to the shrines of the city; those lords and princes who remained at court had perforce to stay, or risk their souls and the souls of their followers as they fled homeward.

The Rose was ready. The city's defenders were armed and in place. The forces that the Lord Protector had sent out were secure, hidden in towns and villages beyond the ring of the siege, awaiting his word.

Armies had to eat, after all—even an army without will or soul. In a day or three or ten, as their lines of supply dwindled one by one, the besiegers would find themselves besieged.

Lutèce had an odd echo to it. The orders of mages were gone, corrupted or fled. Their mother houses were empty; their initiates had vanished. Only the Rose remained, and a few acolytes or initiates of the Isle; and here and there a witch or a diviner or an herb-healer—a power too small or undisciplined to submit to an order, and too stubborn to run.

The city was under siege, body and soul. And yet with the orders gone, the wild magic had begun to rise—which might not have been the enemy's intention, and certainly was not Bernardin's. It shimmered in shadows. It cast bits of glamour across the towers and spires, and rose up out of the river in strange finned shapes.

Not all the gargoyles on the cathedral's towers were made of stone, and not all the creatures that chattered and flocked in the air were birds. They were few still, and cautious; mostly Gereint saw them in the early morning or in the shadows of evening.

But they were there. They filled the empty places that the orders had left. Where there should have been darkness and fear, they brought light and giddy joy.

In the newborn mother house of the Rose, the wild magic did not dare to come. It wanted to: Gereint felt it yearning toward him. But it was not strong enough to withstand such fierce and sharp-edged magic as lived within those walls.

He stood in the armory while the master armorer himself measured the length and breadth of him. He had had armor before, but never made to measure; this was to be his own.

As a Squire, he was entitled to it, but it was a strange, uncomfortable feeling. This was a war, and at last he would be fighting in it. He had been training for it since he came into the order, but this made it real.

There was grief in it, too. Riquier should have been here, chaffing him gently for the great gawk that he was, and assisting the master with his measuring. Instead it was a Squire whom Gereint knew less well, a tall and quiet young man named Arnaud.

Gereint did not begrudge his presence, but it was difficult not to wish it had been Riquier. He welcomed the distraction of a new presence—even though the one who came was altogether unexpected.

The Lady Darienne was alone, plainly dressed, and apparently unperturbed by such martial surroundings. Master Herluin bent his head stiffly but did not pause in his work. Arnaud tried to do the same, but his face was bright red.

They left the courtesies, such as they were, to Gereint. It was faintly humiliating to have to do it while standing with his legs spread wide and one arm up, but he supposed he was up to the task. "Lady," he said. "It's an honor."

"I'm sure it is," she said. "Messires, when you're done with him, I'll borrow him, if I may."

Master Herluin grunted. Arnaud busied himself rather frantically with the last of the measurements. Gereint hoped those were not too far off the mark; his armor would need room to grow in—but not too much.

They finished a bit sooner than they might have otherwise. Gereint had to dress in front of the lady, which should not have troubled him: she was as old as his mother, and had much the same air about her. But she was a stranger, and a Lady of the Isle at that. He caught himself blushing nearly as fiercely as poor Arnaud.

She was not inclined to linger in the armory, which might have been a mercy and might not. Her glance indicated that he was to escort her.

There was an art to it, which he had not mastered even as well as the art of the sword. But she was patient, and if she was almost amused, that did not sting too badly.

They did not go far. The room in which they stopped was full of books, though it had more an air of a study than a library. Parts of it were painfully new, and parts bore signs of none too distant violence: a pillar cracked nearly through, the flags of the floor blackened as if with fire.

Gereint was terribly distracted: he had seen the books and the odd patchwork quality of the room, but it was a long moment before he realized that there were more than books here. In chests and boxes along the walls and among the shelves of books were other things, stranger things, works of magic packed away with care. They were warded, some with great strength, but that meant as little to him as it ever did.

He backed slowly toward the door. "No, Lady. Not here."

"Stay," she said with such an edge of command that he stopped in spite of himself.

"You don't understand, Lady," he said. "I'm not safe around this much magic."

"Then it's time you learned to be," she said.

That was a proper, if gentle rebuke. His teeth clicked together. The mingled magics in this place made his skin twitch, but he dared not damp them. There was no telling what would happen if he tried.

She made him sit in the middle of them, which was a bold thing and a mad thing and a thing none of the Knights would dare. He braced himself for the eruption.

It never came. His skin still twitched; he kept wanting to sneeze. But his magic stayed within the bonds he had set on it.

Darienne nodded as if she had expected no less. She sought out the chest farthest from the door, spoke a word over it that made the air hum and then go still, and lifted the lid.

From the treasures within, she chose one: a simple thing to look at, a lens of glass suspended in a fretwork of silver. Gereint knew that it had to have been a work of years and deep learning, or it would not be here, salvaged from the ruin of the Rose.

She set it on the table in front of him. It reflected the deep blue of her gown, like the night sky between stars, but there was no sign of her face. "We are in perilous straits," she said. "The Knights are bound by their duties and obligations, and stretched vanishingly thin in defense of this realm. They hope to break the siege and crush the enemy between their two forces, but they may not have the strength."

"I know we don't," Gereint said. "Bernardin and his commanders are fighting a brave fight, but the enemy is greater even than we feared. We're monstrously outnumbered."

"That doesn't appear to frighten you."

"It would if I stopped to think," he said. "We need a miracle. But more than anything, we need our queen—and the thing she carries."

"There may be a way," said Darienne. "What you have with her has never been equaled, but there are spells and workings that bring the Rose and the Isle together. Perhaps, to some small degree, I may be able to be to you as she was—enough to find her and bring her back."

Gereint had learned through hard schooling to accept no gift as it was given. There was always a price. "Does my commander know of this?"

"He will."

"Before or after it's done?"

"Which would you prefer?"

"I would prefer," he said, "that all of you learn to see the world as it truly is."

"I think we are beginning to," she said.

"You may not like what you see," said Gereint. "It's not the magic you were taught, or the world you thought you understood."

She regarded him with so calm an expression that he could not bear it. He reached into the well of power and drew up the wild magic.

The room caught fire. It was no mortal flame; it glowed green and blue and gold and silver. Living things danced in it. They knew no rigidity of order, no bonds of earthly workings. They were magic pure.

She was stronger than he had thought. She neither flinched nor tried to drive back that eruption of perfect

"It doesn't matter," said Gereint. "You can't help. It's brave of you to try, but you can't. No one can. Go, please, Lady, and lend your powers to the Rose. Keep Lutèce alive. Let me do what I must do."

"Child," said Darienne, "you are brave, too, and a perfect fool. We'll go in the morning. Can you wait as long as that?"

"Tonight," he said, "as soon as it's full dark."

She sighed. He still had enough of her in him to feel how she regretted that it was winter, and cold, and would be colder once the sun was gone. He felt her flash of guilt, too, and wry amusement at her own weakness. She had lived too long in comfort.

He had come to trust her, as she had intended. He found himself liking her, too. She was like Averil, and like his mother, a little. She would deal honorably with him, as far as she could. In this crumbling world, that was no small thing.

wildness. Her eyes had narrowed, as if she studied it—or him.

He let it go. It sank back into the well from which it had come. Parts of it, glimmering winged creatures like fiery dragonflies, declined to return. They fluttered among the beams of the ceiling; some slipped through the door and escaped.

The world was slightly brighter for their presence in it. Gereint looked into Darienne's eyes. They were wide, but he could not tell if she was awed or appalled.

While he let the magic do its work, he had understood something. "I have to go," he said. "There's no more time left."

"You can't go alone," she said.

"I can't wait for anyone," said Gereint. "It's all coming to a single, devastating point. Can you see? Can you feel it?"

"I see that one man alone, even a mage of such power as yours, can do nothing against what faces us. You will find her, I'm sure of it, but what then? She'll be guarded by the enemy's strongest forces. If he discovers what you are, he'll trap you, corrupt and then destroy you. All that we've done and been and hoped for will be gone."

"There isn't any hope," Gereint said. "And that sets me free. Once I find her, once I win through to her, we'll become a thing he never expects. We'll have a chance, however feeble, to cast him down."

"Let me help you," she said.

"I'd be glad of it, if there were time. There isn't any left. I can't wait for you to break down the walls of magic and belief that you've lived in all your life. I have to be what I am, now, without hesitation. Lady, with all respect, I don't think you're ready for it."

"I can try," said Darienne.

She believed that she could do it. Gereint had to believe, too, or they would both fail.

She lifted the lens that glimmered between them through all their council. It glinted as it moved, dazzling Gereint briefly; he blinked and shook his head. If this was a trap and a new betrayal—

Her eyes met his through the enchanted glass. It was not the same binding of souls as he had with Averil; that was so deep as to be part of himself. This was like scrying: he could see, even feel, what was in her, and know what she knew, as she chose to share it.

She had secrets; he saw walls and locked doors. They were not high or thick and the locks, to his perception, were not particularly strong. Without prying, he could sense whether those secrets pertained to him or to Averil.

It seemed they did not. What the Lady did show him was not what he would call open or honest, but it had the clarity of truth.

She meant to use him. That was no surprise. He was strong, if imperfectly trained, and he was bound to the queen in ways that she intended to study long and deeply. She saw him as a weapon, a great working of magic that might turn on the hand that wielded it.

That was rather precisely what he was. He looked into that mind which was like a house of glass and shadowed crystal, and knew he could shatter it.

Instead he brought light—with great care lest he blind

her. He gave her a little of his strength; only a trickle, again lest he destroy her. It took all the discipline he had, and all the skill, and still she gasped and swayed.

He drew back in despair. "I'm sorry," he said. "I'm hurting you."

She shook her head. She was pale and unsteady, but her determination was as strong as ever. "Give me time—a day. Let me prepare, now I know what to prepare for."

"Another day?" he said. "More delay? More time for the king's dog to eat this kingdom alive?"

"You may rush in, messire, and be eaten alive. Or you may cultivate patience."

"I know where she is," he said.

That gave her pause. There was even a flash of anger, quickly and thoroughly suppressed. "You know? And you said nothing?"

"She wasn't there before," he said. "She is now. Wherever they were hiding her, they've brought her where the wild magic can find her."

"Yet you still can't touch her."

Gereint's heart twisted. He had been holding himself together—rather well, he thought. Darienne's words threatened to shatter him. "If I can get close enough—if I can come to her where she is—"

"You know it must be a trap," said Darienne.

"They don't know what we are," he said. "I don't think they can see wild magic, or understand what it is. It's too quick for them."

"Even so," she said, "if she is where any magic can find her, she is bait, and the hunter is waiting."

17

THE SERVANTS WHO had waited on Averil when she
was in the hunting lodge before were still there,
but Gamelin had made sure of them. It wrenched
her heart to see those eyes empty of will or self. They were
perfect servants, flawless in every respect—except that
there was no living soul in them.

That was the world Gamelin would make. She let Esteban see her anger as they dined by the fire in the hall. She
had touched none of the delicacies on her trencher, nor
done more than sip at the wine. "This is beyond hope of
forgiveness. I ask you, messire: if a lord needs to strip his
followers of souls in order to assure that they will serve
him, is he a lord worth following?"

"I have asked that question myself, lady," said Esteban.
"We do need him; his sorceries have served us well, and when
the Great One wakes, he has the spells that will preserve us
from its wrath. But once that is done and the world is re-
made, he will pay for what he has done. That, I promise you."

"And you will not, messire? In my world, we're taught to
blame the wielder and not the instrument."

"Ah: so every man who takes up a sword is a murderer?"

"Only if he uses it to kill." Averil thrust plate and cup aside and went to stand by the fire. The heat of it seared her cheeks; if she had stood even a hair closer, her skirts would have begun to smolder.

She welcomed the not-quite-pain. "He takes souls away, messire. Does that not trouble you at all?"

"It haunts my dreams," he said, and she did believe him. "I'll pay a price, lady; have no doubt of it. But to bring the new world, that is worth even this. The Church teaches, after all, that souls are born only to die, and their true home is in heaven with the good God. Our ally simply hastens their return."

Averil spun about. "You don't know? You really don't know? Or do you simply refuse?"

He seemed as innocent as he could be: baffled face, lifted hands. She almost could trust that it was real. "What should I know?"

"He is not freeing their souls," Averil said. She wanted to hit him, to pummel the words into him, but she held herself in check. "He is taking them and binding them. Some he destroys. Others he keeps—to feed the Serpent when it wakes, I would presume, though there may be another working we don't know of."

"No," said Esteban, but it was not denial of what she had said. It was realization—terrible and, it seemed, devastating. "No, not that of all spells. He's evil, but he's not mad."

"Would you care to wager on that?" she asked.

"I wish I could," said Esteban. He lowered his head into

his hands. "Oh, by the old gods. I have been worse than a fool."

"Why? What have you done?"

He looked up. He was laughing as a man does when the alternative is to howl at the moon. "There is a spell, lady, that few know of and none dares to work. It forges a chain of souls, binds them with the power of the dead who in life were mages. It destroys the sorcerer who works it—but there is a tale, so ancient it's nigh forgotten, that one sorcerer succeeded; he worked the spell and lived. He lived, in fact, forever."

"So," said Averil, "it makes a man immortal."

"So it seems, but that was not its intended purpose. It was meant to give him the powers of a god."

Averil drew a slow breath. Gods took their power from the souls who worshiped them. If souls were taken, bound, compelled, what could a sorcerer not do?

"He'll wake the Serpent," she said, "and make it his slave. Then he will be the god whom all must worship or be destroyed."

Esteban nodded. His face was stark. "Lady, truly, I did not know."

"You didn't want to know."

"We're all blind in our various ways."

That was true—of Averil as well as any of the rest.

"Lady," said Esteban, "I believe with all my heart that the world will be the better for the Great One's coming. We must not allow my erstwhile ally to fulfill his purpose. Will you help me?"

"I should let you destroy each other," Averil said. "Why should I want any part of either of you?"

"If you were queen in the Great One's world," said Esteban, "you would do great good, and protect your people."

"I can do more good as queen in this world," she said.

"Can you? Can anyone see what you are or what you can do? Or will they rise up in revolt when they realize that your power comes from the wild magic?"

There, thought Averil, was a scrap of honest manipulation. Esteban wanted her safe in his hands and no other's, blindly subject to his will.

She turned her back on him. She was homesick, suddenly, powerfully, for Gereint's presence in body and spirit; for his warmth and his strength and his gift for knowing what words or actions would serve them best.

It was a cold and bitter world without him. Even the pendant on her breast was icy, though she stood close to the fire.

A light hand stroked her hair, traveling downward to her nape and out along her shoulder. She shivered, but lacked the will to shake it off.

"Lady," said Esteban in his warm deep voice. "Join with me; help me. Win back your magic."

"Help you to free the Serpent?" she asked. "Or destroy the sorcerer?"

"Both," he said.

Oh, he played it well, this game of revelation and remorse. Averil wished she could believe that it was true—that he had only just discovered what to her was blindingly obvious.

Even more, she wished that she could cast defiance in his face, blast him and trample him and escape from it all. But she was trapped here. She had to play this game, and pray that her choices did not destroy them all.

"I will help you cast down the sorcerer," she said carefully, "but for a price. Whatever comes of it, however well or badly it ends, I will marry no one by force—not you, not anyone."

"Will you marry willingly?"

"I don't know that I want to marry at all."

He hesitated, which she supposed was a compliment. "By law you must," he said.

"If between us we make a new world," said Averil, "that law will fall with all the rest. I will choose for myself whether to marry, to take a lover, to remain alone—there will be no compulsion. That is the world I would make."

"I could live in such a world," he said.

"Could you?" She turned to face him. He was standing so close she was almost in his arms.

She slid away before he could close the embrace. He was wise enough not to pursue her.

The queen's consort would be a man of great power, whichever world he lived in. He wanted that. He wanted her. That was flattering, even now and even knowing the truth of what he was.

Once she might have wanted him, a little. He was good to look at; he might be slippery when it came to lesser matters, but he made no pretense of being anything but what he was. Of all the men of her own kind who had come seeking her hand, he was the only one she had found even slightly tolerable.

She wanted more than tolerable. If she had to be bound until death to a son of Paladins, she wanted—needed—a strong ally and friend; a true consort, to stand beside her and fight with her and be her match.

Esteban the Morescan was not her match, however fondly he might fancy that he was.

If that fancy served her, she was not above making use of it. That was a sin, and would condemn her in whatever afterlife in which she found herself. But she could pay the price, if it robbed the sorcerer of a potent ally.

"Tell me," she said. "Are you the false priest's new Clodovec? Are there others? Is it only Lys, or is he corrupting the world?"

She held her breath. She had no skill in this game; he would see through her, surely, and laugh in her face.

It seemed she succeeded after all, or he chose to let her succeed. He answered as she had hoped. "He only needs Lys to rule us all. The nine of us whom you have met are with him, but the rest wait upon this kingdom and what passes here."

"He needs me," Averil said, "and what I carry. I am the one he would make his puppet."

"He'll be yours instead," said Esteban.

"Brave words," Averil said. "Foolish, while I have no magic. I hope you know what he did with it."

"I was there," Esteban said. "I marked the working of the spell, and I've studied how to break it. But we have to be careful. He watches always, and listens sometimes. We can't be too hasty, or he'll know."

"Then when?"

"Soon," he said.

"Tonight."

"I don't know—"

"Tonight," she said again.

He bowed. He made no promise, but she could tell: she had him. If it could be done, he would do it.

This must be what it was to seduce a man. She did not like the way it felt, or the need that drove it.

Need forced her to accept it as she did the rest—because she must.

18

GEREINT DID A quite dishonorable thing: he prepared to leave well before sunset. He had no doubt the Lady Darienne was right; he should not go alone. But he could hardly ask anyone else to die with him.

When he came out of the stable leading the horse he had chosen—a sturdy cob with a little speed and much stamina—a delegation was waiting for him. They were all mounted as he intended to be, and dressed the same, too: no armor but a coat of light mail under a cotte as plain as the horses, and no baggage but what they could carry.

He stopped, and wondered if he dared laugh. All his clever plotting, and to them it had been as clearest glass. He was no match for any of them.

Darienne was no surprise, nor Ademar, much. But Mauritius dressed and mounted like the rest—that took Gereint aback. "Messire! You can't go. They need you here."

"The Lord Protector has it all in hand," Mauritius said.

"But—"

"Messire," said the Knight Commander, "if we fail, there will be nothing left to defend. I go where I'm needed most."

Gereint had been trying not to think of what this meant. He would find Averil, he would free her from captivity, he would—what? Save the world?

He wanted her safe and free, and Lys the same. He wanted souls back in bodies and sorcery buried deep and truly forgotten. He wanted the Serpent so sound asleep it would never wake for any spell or raising of powers.

He wanted a great deal, but it was simple in the end. He wanted Averil where she belonged, back inside him. He was withering away without her.

These three had wants and reasons of their own. One of them, he realized as he looked from face to face, was a desire to keep Gereint alive and well. It was not only for his magic, either. They were friends. They would fight beside him, and die if need be. They would risk their souls to keep him safe.

"You can't," he said. "Messires, Lady, you cannot. I can't let you. Either I will win through and find my queen and give her what she needs, or I will die. Nothing that any of you can do will help or change that."

"We beg to differ," said Mauritius. In and around the soft words, Gereint felt the raising of wards, bindings much stronger than one Knight, Master though he might be, could raise.

No one of them was as strong as Gereint. But together, they were a fair match.

They stood poised, waiting for the blow. Gereint could

blast them. It would break them all and maybe break him, too, but he would be free.

They knew as well as he that he could not do that. Dead here or dead in the Wood—what did it matter, after all?

Damn them for loving him. Damn him for being too weak to stop them.

He turned his back on them and flung himself into the saddle. Behind him, though he tried not to listen, he heard the creak and jingle of leather and bit as they followed suit.

The sky was grey, threatening snow yet again, but they did not have far to ride. Half a day—the rest of this day and into the night, now; Gereint did not need light to find the other half of himself.

He led, they followed. The earth guided him. The veins of magic in it were clearer, the lower the sun sank. He bound himself to the deepest and the most difficult to see, but it was the truest of them all.

Although he followed magic, he wielded none of his own. He made himself as invisible as he could, barely even a ripple in the currents that ran so thick and fast all through and around the city.

The streets were empty with the fall of dusk. No one went abroad without dire need. Even the poor and the reckless huddled in what shelter they could find.

The city guard manned the walls on this winter night, a ring of lanterns visible only from within. It was meant to reassure. It served only to remind any who saw, that the enemy's noose had drawn in tight, and the last, desperate game had begun.

Mauritius' rank won the riders through a postern gate,

past guards who held to the raw edge of courage. Clearly they thought the Knight and his companions were mad, but they were bound to obedience. They sent the riders, as they thought, to their certain deaths.

Most likely that was true. It did not stop any of them.

TONIGHT THE GREATER roads were barred by silent armies, and the twelve bridges over the river were no longer open to any who passed. But there were gaps in the wall of flesh and steel, lesser tracks and forgotten byways that ran along the river and crossed it far from the city, or else wound away into the fields and forests of the kingdom.

The enemy did not care if a few stragglers escaped. The Rose, by duty and honor, would never retreat. Once he had destroyed them, Lutèce would be his, with all its magic and its well of power.

Gereint dared to hope that, even yet and in spite of all else that he knew, the sorcerer either did not know or did not reckon the worth of what Gereint was to the captive queen. If he looked at all, let him see a party of stragglers in the winter night, making their shivering way out of the beleaguered city.

The Golden Wood lay north and west of Lutèce. The road to it was heavily guarded. Even with his magic tightly bound, Gereint could feel the heavy dark mass of the army lying like a leaden weight on the earth.

He rode warily along the river, reining in the desperate impatience that would have sent him galloping straight into the sorcerer's claws. The Wood was calling him, but he took care to follow the currents in the earth, away from the armies and down paths that were still clean of Serpent magic.

It was painfully slow going. He paused often, all his senses at the alert. Nothing human or animal was out tonight in the dark and the cold, but the rattle of branches or the sigh of wind might signify something ominous.

Not long after the soft snow began to fall, Gereint stopped yet again. The wind had died. Nothing moved anywhere. And yet he thought he had heard . . .

There. Again. His horse's head was up, ears pricked. He slid from the saddle and covered the gelding's nostrils with his hand, lest a snort betray them all.

There was no moonlight or starlight, but a glimmer of light broadened on the track ahead of them. A half-substantial, half-unreal shape stepped delicately out from among the trees that grew close by the river there.

It looked like a fox, a delicate silvery creature such as ran the hills in the distant north. Foxes were not entirely of mortal earth in any case, but this one was even less so than most.

It sat and wrapped its tail neatly around its feet. Its yellow eyes laughed at the mortals on their big lumbering horses, trying to skulk and creep and hide.

They should stop trying to be Knights, and study the ways of foxes. The silver fox did not know if it was inclined to teach them. It had come looking for the great magic that sang in the heart of things, and found it buried inside a worthless lump of a human body.

Gereint felt the sting of that appraisal, but he was well accustomed to being disapproved of. "Show us how to be foxes," he said.

The fox tilted its head. The ways of a fox were intricate and subtle and needed more patience than humans were capable of. They would fail; the enemy would find them and do what it had done to all the rest of the humans it caught.

The vision the fox gave Gereint was devastatingly apt. Wherever the sorcerer's armies were, the fox saw nothing. Darker than darkness, utterly empty, they took all the light out of the world.

"Help us bring it back," Gereint said.

The fox did not think it could work such a miracle. But, like all its kind, it loved a good hunt. The more discomfited the hunters happened to be, the better the fox liked it.

It rose with a flick of the tail, turned, and not quite vanished into the wood. The humans could follow or not. It did not care.

That not-caring was part of the lesson. Gereint felt as much as heard the others treading softly in his wake, leading their horses as he did.

Briefly he considered sending the beasts home and continuing on foot, but they might yet prove useful. They were quiet and obedient, almost preternaturally so.

He had walked often before on the borders between worlds. This was a little different. He never left the mortal world, but on the fox's trail, he was not quite of it. He walked where the wild magic walked, slipping through trees that kept still a few rags of autumn gold.

It was a long and circuitous way. Gereint resisted the temptation to lose himself in the blind act of following. He kept his senses as sharp as they could be; he marked each turn and doubling, and as often as not, marked the cause of it, too: a clot of blackness that sucked the soul out of anything that passed.

Not every such shadow was the sorcerer's doing. A fair few proved to be shrines or churches, and one of the worst looked to be an abbey.

To the wild magic, both orders and Serpent were equally deadly. The fox slipped through the narrow spaces between them.

Gereint's companions were so silent that he could almost forget their presence. Mauritius and the Lady at least must understand what he was doing. It was a miracle, almost, that they offered no objection.

Maybe the world could change after all.

The dark places were closer together now, and it took longer and was more difficult to evade them. At last, when the taste of dawn was in the air, there was no way to go but forward, but that way was as black as the sorcerer's heart.

The fox went to earth. It was small and more than half magical; for it, the art was both simple and swiftly accomplished.

Four human creatures and four horses stood forsaken in the wood, while the snow fell thick and fast. A good half-thousand of the sorcerer's soldiers camped in the valley ahead of them. On one side rose a steep ridge; on the other ran a swift torrent of a river.

Both ridge and river guarded the heart of the Wood. The paths of power ran straight beneath them.

For the first time since this strange journey began, Darienne spoke. "You've led us well, messire, but now I think it's time we earned our keep."

"Lady—" Gereint tried to say.

"We're not as useless as you may think," Mauritius said dryly.

Gereint flushed. "Messire, Lady, I didn't mean—"

"The world may change," said Darienne, "and we may change with it. Be quiet now, in your whole self. Remember the fox, and the mist and the fog, and the rain that falls soft in the night."

Her voice had a subtle rhythm, almost a chant. It fit the movement of branches in the wind, and the dance and swirl of snow, and the eons-slow breathing of the earth under their feet.

They moved through it as the fox had moved through the wood. Yet instead of trees, they moved down long aisles of tents. Bodies breathed within or stood watch around the edges, oblivious to the storm.

There was no light here, no warmth but the barest sufficiency. There were no words, no singing; even breath came slow, as if the power that animated these bodies begrudged the necessity.

The power wore all these bodies as a serpent wears its scales. Each one was a part of it, and it was aware of each.

Under Darienne's spell, the four invaders were no more than wind blowing through the rows of tents. Gereint admired the subtlety of it, and took care to notice, as she clearly intended, that it was quite like certain workings of the wild magic.

It was all one magic. He trod carefully, leading his horse and doing his best not to break or alter the spell. The fox's magic had been easier to follow; this had odd notes and peculiar disharmonies.

It kept wanting to impose its own order on the wildness around it. The Lady could hardly help it; all her training compelled her to do it. She resisted, and mostly she succeeded. But as she passed the midpoint of the camp, she found it more difficult. The twists and random turns of the magic begged to be turned into clear and coherent patterns.

Gereint had learned not to meddle in the affairs of mages. They did not take kindly to it, and his magic had a way of making matters much worse. But the spell was faltering, and the camp surrounded them, and the will that ruled it had begun to rouse.

He only meant to take the smoothness out of the patterns. He did that, and not badly, either. But her magic fought back.

It was beautiful, as the crystalline planes of glass could be. It rose like a shrine of light in that dark and storm-wracked place.

Gereint swept a veil of darkness over it. But he was too slow. The camp had snapped awake.

He flung Darienne and then Ademar onto their horses. Mauritius, quick-witted as ever, was already mounted and spurring onward.

The enemy's soldiers swarmed over them. They all, even Ademar, abandoned caution. He had a fair hand with a mage-bolt, for a Novice.

They cut a swath through the mass of bodies, but there were always more behind and beside and all about. Gereint dared not blast the lot of them, lest the fire fall on his friends. He aimed beyond them, toward the mind that animated them.

It was not the king's sorcerer. He knew that mind and presence, cold and serpent-supple, underlaid with the hiss of scales. This was human: a mage, and strong, but not as strong as he wished to be.

Gereint stalked him through the minds of his slaves—but swiftly: they had risen like a wave to fall on the Knights and the Lady. Even as Ademar faltered and Mauritius' horse stumbled and fell, Gereint found the target.

He did not strike to kill. He turned all his force against the magic and snuffed it like a candle's flame.

Soulless bodies toppled. Emptied of will, they drained of life as well. The four who were living stood in a field of the dead, while the snow fell with relentless softness.

19

G ORONWY THE PRINCE had always loved secrets, though keeping them was difficult. This was the greatest secret he had ever stumbled upon.

He left Dylan Fawr and his hulking lover to raise such protections as mages of the orders were capable of. They were weak as always, trapped in their rigid boxes. The other magic, the new and wonderful magic, slithered effortlessly around and under and through them.

His teacher had many preoccupations, and more secrets than Goronwy had ever dreamed of keeping. But when Goronwy needed him, some part of him was always there.

At first he had lived in Goronwy's dreams. With time and teaching, Goronwy had learned to make a mirror in which he appeared. It seemed an ordinary mirror, not even a scrying glass, and to mages of the orders it had no discernible magic. It took the new magic to understand what a powerful working it was.

Goronwy kept the secret of the Serpent's tooth for three days, hugged close to his chest, before he approached the mirror. He had had his exercises, his books and spells, to engross him, but no word from the master.

That was not unusual: sometimes he labored alone for days or weeks. Still, this time he felt a difference in his bones. The world was changing in ways he could not yet put words to.

He kept the mirror in the closet of his chamber in the palace, laid with careful casualness in a chest of clothing and oddments. His books of magic, his workings and his potions and his secrets, he shielded with strong wards, but the mirror appeared to have, and need, no protection.

That was an ancient art and subtle, and the world had forgotten it. Goronwy lifted the mirror from its wrappings and held it up for a moment to let it drink the grey winter light that shone through the narrow window.

The mirror was as wide as his two hands held together, and made of bronze, polished until it was as bright almost as gold. A frame of curling bronze tendrils enclosed it; they seemed to be leaves and vines unless one looked closely and found the eyes and scales of serpents.

He closed the chest and propped the mirror against the wall. The door was barred—that had been his first lesson and one of the strongest. No one must know this of all his secrets.

His breath came a little quickly. He knew the spell for summoning the mirror's magic, but he had never worked it before. The master had always summoned him, reaching through the mirror into his heart and mind.

He could wait. The master would come to him again

soon. Prydain had kept this secret for twice a thousand years; Goronwy could keep it for another day or two.

Even as he decided not to perform the working, his hands moved of their own accord to shape the spell. The words were in his mind, flowing to his lips and tongue. The magic had him, and wielded him at its will.

The mirror woke. It did not, like scrying glasses of the orders, stir and shimmer. It opened like an eye and stared straight into Goronwy's heart.

Sometimes he saw the master's face. More often he saw a serpent's eye, yellow-green and slit-pupiled, fixing itself coldly upon him. On this day, he looked into the Serpent's maw, a long dark tunnel that opened to swallow him whole.

He was not the fool most people took him for. He had defenses. But the spell was strong and he was, to a degree, willing. It took the knowledge from him, the secret and all that went with it.

Then he saw the master. He sat at ease in the Serpent's belly, white and naked and faintly but distinctly scaled. His eyes that Goronwy remembered as pale but human enough, were as yellow as the Serpent's own.

He smiled at his student, a smile as pale and cold as his eyes. "Well done, my child. Oh, well done."

In another age, Goronwy would have preened. He was past that now. He bent his head, regally as he hoped, and preserved an equally regal silence.

He could not tell if the master approved. His face grew less human as the moments passed.

Goronwy reflected distantly that he might be wise to be

afraid. He had never seen the master so clearly before. Either it was an honor or it was a death sentence.

"Now, child," the master said, oh so cold and oh so quiet, "I have a task for you. It needs a strong heart and a strong stomach, and magic that never falters. If this is beyond you, say so without fear. It is a dangerous thing I ask, and it could be deadly."

"I'm not afraid," Goronwy said.

That was not exactly true, but he was not so terrified that he could bear to run. He had prepared long and hard for this. From the beginning he had known that the master would use him, as he used the master. This was the reckoning, and he welcomed it—though his heart beat hard and his body trembled.

The master nodded as if both the fear and the willingness pleased him. "Listen, then, and remember."

As A ROYAL prince in Prydain, Goronwy had—he would not say owned—a company of the queen's guard. These were picked men, matched for height and looks, beautifully and impeccably trained. When he was younger, Goronwy had dreamed of becoming one of them.

Now of course he knew he never would. A prince did not become a guardsman, even if he would ever grow tall enough.

He inspected the six whom he had chosen. They were the tallest and the best to look at, and they were all famous fighters. In their carefully expressionless faces he saw both studied patience and not quite concealed contempt.

That faint edge of scorn hardened Goronwy's heart. He

had had doubts of what he was to do. No longer. He had bound himself to change the world.

It began here. He cupped in his hands the working that the master had shown him how to make. For such a terrible thing, it was almost childishly simple: a jar no longer than his smallest finger, made of clay fired in a potter's kiln. The power came from the words incised on it with a serpent's tooth, and the words spoken over it once it had come out of the kiln.

He had made it in a day and a night. It had taken its toll in strength, but that would come back, the master had promised him. He had only to finish the spell, to raise the vessel and say the words that had been burned into his memory.

As with the mirror, he felt the magic take hold. It ripped the words out of him. They hissed in the room.

Nothing happened. His guardsmen stood immobile, resigned to the peculiar behavior of princes.

In his hands, the vessel beat like a heart. Goronwy looked up from it into the guardsmen's eyes.

There was nothing there. They were empty. They lived, breathed, moved at his half-startled, half-incredulous command. They danced for him, because he bade them.

He shuddered. The vessel nearly slid from his fingers. He clamped them shut.

Six tall men capered and cavorted around him with empty faces, empty hearts, empty eyes. "Stop," he said shakily. "For the love of God, stop!"

They stopped and stood perfectly still, as if they had never moved at all. Goronwy stared at them. His breath came hard, as if he and not they had done the dancing.

They were his. All that they were or had been was gone. All that was left was obedience. Everything else beat inside the vessel that he must never lose or break.

He tucked it into the purse at his belt. Strength was coming back, as the master had said. His breathing quieted, and with it his mind.

He had done it, the irrevocable thing, the thing that changed everything. He felt a little different. He was stronger.

"Come," he said to his most loyal and obedient men. And they came, because there was no choice left to them.

THE SPELL WAS only the beginning. The master had urged Goronwy to wait thereafter, and move only when he was certain that he could succeed. Then help would come, allies whom the master had chosen and trained, as he had done with Goronwy.

But Goronwy had an odd feeling in his belly. The queen was a powerful mage. Once she discovered what her nephew had done with the pick of her guard, there would be no time left.

The master had given him the knowledge. It was clear and strong inside him. It led him by ways he had walked before, through the city of Caermor in the rain and wind, into the early dark. But he needed no light to see.

The shrine of the Serpent's tooth loomed before him, seeming taller and more foreboding in the dimness than it ever had in daylight. The wards upon it were stronger than he remembered, the spells more tightly woven. More than a pair of mages stood guard there, surely.

Goronwy held six brave souls captive, and a great master of the old magic had shown him what he must do. He was no feeble mage himself, either, whatever the orders of Prydain might like to believe. Their ways were dying. Goronwy belonged to a newer world.

His men went before him into the church. For all their bulk and the weight of their armor, they moved without sound.

It was as the master had said: wards did not touch them. They had no souls for such magic to find, and no spirits to capture.

They were Goronwy's shield against the shrine's defenses. Even with their protection, those defenses burned and stung. He set his teeth and pushed through.

No alarms rang. No bolts of fire smote him. The high stone space was breathlessly still. The vigil lamp over the altar barely flickered.

Far down inside, he was gibbering with terror. There was no reason for it. No armies defended this place. Its magic could not stand against his. The master had said so.

The master had told him to go down below, to enter the crypt. There was nothing there but old bones and old stone, and a tooth like a milky white dagger.

A woman knelt beside the ancient lady's tomb, with a shimmering veil of magic about her and an air of such royal serenity that Goronwy had halted and bowed before he realized what he did.

The queen herself mounted guard over the treasure of her kingdom. What woke in Goronwy was not so much shock or terror as exultation. He had expected to find Dylan Fawr, or better and more easily yet, young Baron Four-chard. This was a prize beyond any he had hoped for.

His men moved as if they had been part of his body. The queen's defenses crackled over them, but they never faltered.

The first to lay hands on her flamed up like a torch. Goronwy felt the man's dissolution as a rending in his gut. But it did not weaken him. It made him angry.

That anger drove the rest upon her, overwhelmed her magic and struck her down.

Goronwy's shock at his own strength nearly undid him, as he stood gaping at the queen of Prydain lying uncon-scious at his guardsmen's feet. Memory of the master's voice hissed in his ears, driving him onward as he had driven his own men.

The Serpent's tooth gleamed beneath its veil of magic. Goronwy gathered himself for the last stroke, which was perhaps most difficult of all. He had spent magic without care for the cost, trusting in the vessel of souls that rode so uneasily in his purse.

Now he must spend it all if need be. He called every scrap of power he had, and all the knowledge he had gained from his lessoning with the master. Any part of him that had been weak or inclined to doubt, he closed off. Even the part that would cast scorn back in the faces of everyone who had ever sneered at him or called him weakling or coward or worse, he crushed down and forcibly forgot. His whole world was this spell, in this place, in this moment.

The words must be spoken perfectly, in a language that had been old when the first human creature spoke the first human word. Much of it was a modulation of hisses.

The master's memory was in him, the master's voice speaking through him. He was a perfect instrument—but he kept his soul. He intended never to lose it.

The veil shuddered and darkened to black, but the tooth shone through it. As the last word died in hissing silence, Goronwy struck the darkness with his fist.

Burning cold pierced him through. He had never known such pain. It seared his magic and gripped his soul.

Six souls swirled within their vessel, battering the sides, desperate to escape. Their desperation fed Goronwy, gave him strength to battle past the pain.

It was a bitter fight. It nearly stripped Goronwy of memory as of everything else. But with the last of his self, he heard the master's voice, speaking soft and clear amid the torrent of fire. "Pain is illusion. Fear has no substance. Forget them both. Be pure will and pure power. Take the tooth, and all of it will stop."

His body was a dim and distant thing. It was a great journey and a terrible effort to reach through the storm of icy fire and find his hand, then lay his will upon it. He could not do it; he was too weak. He had always been weak. He always would be.

No. It was not a word, really. It was a force: pure refusal, and stubbornness straight down to the bone. These bones, this hand, closed around the Serpent's tooth.

The storm went still. Slowly but perceptibly the pain faded. Goronwy stood in the silent crypt, staring down at the effigy of a woman, a queen: twice a traitor while she lived, and now, in death, the salvation of the Great One whom she had served and then betrayed.

The tooth was cool and smooth in his hand. It too had gone quiet. He shivered a little at the thought of what it was, but all the fear had been burned out of him.

He slipped it into his purse beside the vessel of souls. His guardsmen, less the one whose body the queen had killed, were waiting on his will.

He paused, frowning. She was alive, though both life and magic burned low. He bent to snuff them out, but straightened again with the task undone.

The master would not be pleased. But Goronwy could not do it. If that made him weak and a fool, then so be it.

He left her where she lay, tangled with the body of the guardsman. She no longer mattered, he told himself, now that her treasure was taken, and he had a journey to make. The sooner he began it, the sooner the world would change.

Then nothing that mattered now would matter at all, and everything would be different. Better, he thought. Better by far than it could possibly be now.

20

IT WAS MORE than a single night before Esteban brought Averil's magic back to her. She counted three days of unrelenting tedium, alone but for the soulless servants and the guards who barred every door and window and every thought she had of slipping away.

There was a library of sorts, a chest in the solar that held a handful of saints' lives, a history of old Romagna, and a treatise on the art of cookery. Whoever had written that last had had a particular affinity for wild game—appropriate enough for a hunting lodge.

Averil had no deer or boar to cook, and her captors would not even let her out into the stable, let alone into the wood to hunt. She read each book through twice, escaped briefly to the kitchen but found it too eerily silent with its empty-eyed cooks and speechless servants.

Hour upon hour she tried to reach her magic. She slept, and hoped to dream it back, or find Gereint somewhere amid the shadows. But even dreams eluded her. Her sleep was heavy and dark, and when she woke, she felt as if she had not slept at all.

By the morning of the fourth day, she was ready to wrest a sword from a guard's scabbard and throw herself on it. As the servant brought her breakfast of bread sopped in watered wine, she darted past him.

The door was barred as she had expected. She lunged at the two men who stood in her way. She had no thought for strategy or finesse. Her whole eye and mind focused on the dagger at the nearer man's belt. It was nearly as long as a sword. She wrenched it free and stabbed.

The blade sank deep in his side, but he stood unmoving, as solid and impervious as the wall.

He might feel no pain, but he was fast, and strong. His hands gripped like iron. She went briefly mad, twisting, biting, scratching.

It was like doing battle with a fencepost.

"Let her go," Prince Esteban said.

The door was open and he was in it. So close, that freedom, and so far away.

Averil hung in the guardsman's hands. When he dropped her, she was prepared. She staggered but kept her feet.

She was flushed, disheveled, breathing hard. Esteban's raised brow took note of it all and politely refrained from judgment.

"I beg your pardon, lady," he said. "I was unavoidably detained."

"I do not wait well," she said, biting off each word.

"I shall remember that," said Esteban.

Empty-eyed soldiers followed him into the hall, taking station wherever she might think to escape. The man she had stabbed crumpled then, as if the arrival of the rest had freed him to succumb to his wound.

No one moved to stanch the bleeding or to restore the life that streamed out of him. Averil hissed at them all and dropped to her knees.

As she pressed the hem of the man's own cloak to the wound, Esteban said, "It's no mercy to keep him alive as he is. Let him go."

Averil knew Esteban was right. She hated him for it, and for the evil that had made this man what he was. "Tell me you can give me back my magic," she said.

"I can try," said Esteban.

That was not precisely encouraging. Averil bound up the wound, bandaging it with strips of wool from the man's cloak, cut with the dagger that had stabbed him. No one helped her, but no one hindered, either.

When she had done the best she could for him, she pushed herself to her feet. "Now try," she said to Esteban.

He had gone somewhat pale. "Not here," he said. "Come with me."

SHE THOUGHT HE would take her back down into the cavern, but he led her down the corridor to a room thick with dust and disuse, that must once have been a chapel. Its altar and its furnishings were gone, but the faint scent of incense hung about it still.

Even in this dulled world in which she lived now, she could feel the remnants of holiness that clung to the walls. Kings and queens had prayed here. Those prayers, like incantations, had sunk into the stones.

The windows still held their treasure of enchanted glass. That surprised Averil a little: so much else had been taken away from this place. But when she looked up into the images that shone sunlit above her, she understood.

As with the Mystery that she wore around her neck, what at first seemed a pattern of leaves and vines resolved itself into a coil of serpents. There was the great Tree of the world, and the Serpent coiled around its trunk and through its branches.

An image very like it shone in the Chapel Perilous of the Isle. Here as there, Averil marked how the Serpent seemed neither evil nor deadly, but ancient and subtle and wise.

This world held so many secrets. All the things that she had thought she knew, all the sureties, all the things she had been taught as truth, had proved to be far other than they seemed. Her own blood was not what she had been raised to believe; she was the child not of loyal and saintly Madeleine but of the great traitor, the Lady Melusine.

And yet that was a lie, too. Melusine had been no traitor. She had served the Serpent at the Young God's behest, taught it to trust her, then helped him strike the blow that cast it down and bound it in enchanted sleep.

Maybe that was a lie, too. Maybe no one knew the truth. Averil had lost her trust in anything that mortals taught.

She turned to Esteban. She did not trust him, either, but she needed him.

He had come alone into the chapel. His guards stood without, and probably ringed the walls, but none of them was in sight.

Maybe he was a prisoner, too. She trusted him no more for it, but her dislike softened ever so slightly.

He approached her and reached for her hands. She stepped back. He pursued. She raised the knife that was still in her hand.

"Lady," he said with courtesy that she had to admire in such circumstances, "for the working we must touch. Please; there's not much time."

Averil eyed him warily but let him take the hand that did not hold the dagger. He might not need the warning, but she needed the reassurance.

He was wise enough not to argue. He led her into the light that poured from the window onto the floor. Even in her muffled state, Averil felt the tingle of the magic on her skin.

The tingle rose to a burning, shot through with sharp small pains like the stings of bees. Esteban's grip was tight enough to bruise.

Pain was a focus. It cast Averil deep into her body, turned her awareness inward and sharpened it until there was nothing else in the world.

There were walls. There were wards and barriers, shields made of magic that was so alien that it, too, was pain. She made a lens of that pain, a burning glass. It caught the many-colored light of the window and focused it into a single, white-hot beam.

She turned it on the heart of the wards. She fancied she could catch the acrid smell of burning, as if the wards had been living flesh.

The wall around her magic crumbled and fell into ash.

She reeled before the full force of her own power, headlong as a wave of the sea. It swept her up as if to bear her away.

She scrambled for every scrap of discipline she had ever had, every vestige of control. Even as she did it, she wavered on the edge of despair. She was both too strong and too weak. Her enemy, her captor, was rousing.

He had sensed the disturbance in the spell. Somewhat wildly she flung up wards, pulling strength from she hardly cared where—earth, air, sky, wild magic, it did not matter.

It succeeded. The enemy's consciousness withdrew. The tide of magic abated. It was stronger still than she liked, and less obedient than she wanted it to be. But it was hers again. She was as whole as she could be, with that last wall still immovable, dividing her from the half of her self.

That would not give way for any force she laid on it. It was a working of its own, and she could not understand it. It should have broken with the rest.

This should not be. Gereint should be there, should be inside her. The spell was broken. She was herself again—except for that. And that meant she had won very little at all.

She had her magic, such as it was without him. She opened her eyes to Esteban's face.

He was white and shaking; his eyes flinched from hers. He looked as if he had come to the end of his strength.

There was no chair or couch for him to sit on. She coaxed him down to the floor. He did his best to descend with grace, but his knees buckled; he dropped with force enough to startle a gasp out of him.

She fed him a trickle of her own strength, until he could sit upright. He drew a ragged breath. "I . . . thank you."

"It's I who owe you thanks," she said. "Come now. We have the night at most before your ally realizes what he's lost. We'd best use it."

Even in the state Esteban was in, he looked at her with a kind of sardonic hope. She was almost sorry to dash it. "I take it you have a plan," she said.

"I—" He swallowed, then rose unsteadily to his feet. "Yes. We must be swift. Come, lady."

Averil did not live to obey his command, but for the moment they were allies. She paused to savor the fire of magic that burned strong in her, and to make certain that no hostile power could detect it.

Then she was ready. She inclined her head to Esteban. He bowed in return and took her hand.

His hand barely trembled. Hers was perfectly steady. She was beyond fear, cherishing the heat of anger that held the lesser emotions at bay.

If Gamelin could be destroyed, she would destroy him. That vow she swore to herself in the silence of her heart.

21

G EREINT WAS LOST in the snow. The field of the twice dead lay behind him; the wood was all about him, an unending wilderness of trees.

His companions rode in silence, offering no guidance. They seemed stunned, or else lost in a dream. That was as he had feared: mages of the orders did not thrive outside of their meticulous and beautifully wrought boxes.

As dark closed in, he surrendered to necessity and halted. They had no tents and precious little baggage, but a copse of trees up against a shelf of cliff offered shelter and wood for a fire.

They made camp without speaking, built the fire and tended the horses and ate what they had in their saddle-bags: bread, cheese, a handful of barley that, boiled in melted snow, made a sturdy if tasteless gruel.

Darienne passed round a flask of cordial that tasted like sunlight and made Gereint's head spin. She had come back to herself more quickly than either Mauritius or Ademar, but she was as taciturn as they.

Gereint had had enough of silence. Partly under the cordial's influence and partly because he felt he had to say it, he said, "If you want to go back to Lutèce in the morning, go. No one will fault you."

For a long while none of them spoke. Gereint was about to burst out in a fit of sheer temper, when Ademar said in his most world-weary drawl, "We are a frightful disappointment, aren't we? One good look at the enemy and we fall to pieces."

That was painfully true, and Gereint did not try to deny it. He did try to be gentle as he said, "All this time, Lady, messires, you've seen what we all face; you've suffered, you've sacrificed, you've watched those you love die and worse. And yet, time and again, you fall back into your old ways of thinking. You know we all have to change, but you've done nothing to make it happen. Even if we win this war, no part of the world will be the same. Again, you know that, and you've persisted in refusing to act on it."

He paused. It was a miserably uncomfortable thing to say these words to these people. He kept wanting to scrape his feet, duck his head and mumble apologies.

Too late for that now. He swallowed hard and went on. "I didn't ask you to come with me. I don't believe you're useless, but there are things you'll have to accept before you can go on. If you can't accept them, you will leave. I'll not have your lives and souls on my conscience."

"Hard words," Mauritius said: "as hard to speak as to hear, I'm sure. We do deserve them, after all we've seen and done. But, messire, may we try again? Can we still hope to be of some use in this battle?"

"It's going to get worse," Gereint said. "What we saw

back there, what I had to do—that's just the beginning. Ask yourself honestly, messire: can you do what I did? Can you do even more, if need calls for it? Honestly, messire. Do you understand what I did, and how, and why?"

Mauritius took his time in answering. Gereint did not press him. For a mage of his order and power, this was a terrible thing; it went against much that he had been raised and trained to be.

Mauritius knew it. He had known it since after the Rose fell, when he rode away from the Field of the Binding into the Wildlands. He had seen the wild magic then, and taken perforce the help that it offered.

Now he would have to do more. He would have to wield the magic itself.

"Time was," he said as if to himself, "when you would have been cast out of the order for what you are and what you do, and I would be sent down to the filthiest outpost imaginable and reduced to a mere and simple Knight or even a Squire, for the crime of bringing you among us."

"So you would have," Gereint said, "before the Rose fell. Both of us still may, if we win this war. We'll not be doing this for glory, or even for gratitude. We'll do it because there is nothing else we can do."

"That has always been the way with our order," Mauritius said. "Did you ever swear an oath to wield only one kind of magic?"

"No, messire," Gereint said. "But—"

"A Knight is no different, messire. What the order is at its heart and what it's been made to be by time and tradition may not be the same thing."

That was not easy for Mauritius to say. Gereint could hear the effort in it, the wrenching of his mind away from patterns that had ruled it all his life long. It was a great thing he did, as great as any gallantry in battle.

Gereint bowed to it. "I'm honored to have you beside me, messire."

THE WHOLE OF the Wood lay under a spell as convoluted as a nest of serpents. There was no straight path; no way through. Every path they took twisted into another and circled round to where they began.

Even the tracks beneath the earth were muddled and confused. When Gereint tried to follow them, he doubled up, heaving. It was worse than dizziness; it was as if a hand had reached up out of the ground and twisted his gut.

He had never been cut off from the earth before. His magic had never been weakened, either; nothing had ever touched it, even when he wanted it to.

He would not say he was afraid. But he had a little better understanding of his companions.

Now, in turnabout, they were stronger than he. Ademar and Mauritius did turn and turn in the lead, picking their way step by step through the maze. Darienne was the rear guard; she maintained the wards that protected them, and kept watch against the enemy.

For the first time in a long while, Gereint bowed to magic that was both stronger and more skilled than his own. For all the strength that was in him, he was still a raw novice. These were masters of their art, so smooth and sure that they made it seem effortless. They flowed together like a dance.

By the second morning, as they broke camp, the snow ended at last. The sky hung heavy; the air was still and dank and cold. Darienne had labored through the night, working spells with fire and crystal, but the Wood was no more penetrable than it had been since they began.

They had not prepared for a long journey. At worst even Mauritius had calculated to spend two days, maybe three, on the road. Then the horses would need forage and the riders would have to hunt for game, which seemed to have vanished from the Wood.

"I'll wager if we turn back, the road will be open," Ademar said. He managed to sound as if that was not the choice he would make, but they could hardly fail to consider it. Ademar would make a fine courtier, if there was any mortal court left after all this was done.

"If we don't break the spell by morning, we will have to turn back," Mauritius said.

"No," said Gereint. "We can't give up. There isn't enough time."

"And there is time to keep riding in circles? Messire," said Mauritius, "with a company of Knights we may break through this. If we can reach the edge of the Wood and escape the spell's grip, I'll summon all who can ride. They'll be here within a day."

That was a strong temptation, and Gereint nearly succumbed to it. But the prickle of his nape warned him not to trust that sudden surge of hope.

"It won't work," he said. "He doesn't know we're here yet; the spell is blind, and he's not watching it. An army of the Rose will raise every defense he has, and spring the trap."

"We can do that," said Mauritius, "or we can wander till we die. What other choices do we have?"

Gereint had no answer for him. There was one, there had to be, but it kept eluding his grasp.

The others had decided. If they did not find a way through the Wood by sunset, they would pitch camp; then at first light they would go.

As chance would have it, they camped well before sundown, having found a place that seemed both safe and sheltered. The ruins of a stone house offered walls and part of a roof, and protection against wind and snow and prying eyes.

They fed the horses the last of the grain and hobbled them in the clearing where they could paw through the snow to winter-seared grass. For the riders there was a small loaf of bread baked in the coals of the fire, a bit of cheese, and a napkinful of shriveled but remarkably sweet apples that Ademar had found on the clearing's edge, growing in the remnants of an orchard.

The others had not seemed to find that remarkable; old farmsteads were a common enough thing, some as old as Romagna and others lost to various wars in all the years since. But Gereint the farmer's son was oddly perturbed. It was the only such place they had seen since they entered the Wood, and the only place where such trees grew.

He kept thinking of the Wildlands, and the farmstead in which the Knights had rested after they fled from the king's armies, a place of such deep magic that there was no end to it. That place belonged to Peredur, or he to it. It was a refuge of great power and peace.

Gereint did not know why an overgrown orchard and the ruin of a house should remind of him of that other, immortal and indestructible place. Maybe because it was so unlike anything else they had passed. It was an oddity; it was out of place in this wilderness of oak and ash, beech and hazel.

He ate his meager supper, saw to it that the horses were in as much comfort as they could be, and came back to the shelter and the fire. Ademar was already asleep; Darienne, exhausted from her labor the night before, was nodding where she sat. Mauritius kept watch, with the fire as his scrying glass.

Gereint wanted to ask him about the farmstead, but could not think of a way to frame the question so that it made sense. He rolled himself in his cloak instead and closed his eyes. The sun was still up, but not for long. Maybe if he could sleep, his head would be clearer when he woke.

One thing he was sure of. The others could go back. It would be better if they did. But he was going on, no matter what it cost him.

22

GORONWY FLED THE shrine of the Serpent's tooth, running as much from guilt as from danger. His aunt the queen was still alive, but barely. He wanted her dead, but not enough to go back and make sure of her.

He had at most a handful of hours before her servants found her. By then he had to be well away from Caermor. He ran for the river, following the guides that the master had left: sparks of magic that showed him the way.

A ship waited as the master had promised. It was small, black of hull and sail, with a prow like a dragon's head. Its captain was one of the sea-folk, but there was something not quite right about him. He felt twisted somehow, bent out of true.

His sailors had a familiar blankness about the eyes. Goronwy found it reassuring, in its way.

Even as Goronwy's own blank-eyed guards found places out of the way, the captain called on the crew to raise sail. The tide was running on, and a storm was brewing.

Goronwy had no baggage, no provisions, nothing but the

vessel of souls and the Serpent's tooth. There were blankets below, and wine and salt fish and the rock-hard bread that sailors favored. Goronwy was not moved as yet to touch any of them. He returned to the deck and the open air, as the ship came about and rode wind and tide toward the sea.

Strong spells lay on that ship. Caermor's defenses could not touch it, nor did the queen's rivermaster appear to demand an accounting. As the city slid away behind, Goronwy felt as if the world slid with it.

Where he was going, all things were possible. Nothing would ever be the same.

A STORM RAGED at sea. The clouds nearly touched the tops of the waves; the great swell dwarfed the little ship.

But where they sailed, the sea was as smooth as glass. The only wind that touched them was the brisk breeze that filled the sail. They skimmed that narrow path between walls of heaving water, flying more swiftly than mortal winds could carry them.

Goronwy, exhilarated, ascended to the prow. He meant to peer ahead, but as he laid his hand on the dragon's head, he felt not the smooth hardness of painted wood, but something much stranger.

Those slitted golden eyes were alive. Scales curved like beadwork under his palm. They were warm in the winter's cold: there was fire in the dragon's heart.

Goronwy reclaimed his hand with care. Clearly there was more to the master's magic than he had imagined. He wondered, half eagerly and half with apprehension, what he would find when he came to the master himself.

There would be a reward, he was sure. He had captured the key. The throne of Prydain would be the least that he could expect in return.

That was a pleasant daydream. He let it enfold him as the ship flew onward toward the distant shadow of land.

GORONWY HAD LOST track of the time. It was still daylight. Beyond the black wall of cloud, the sun must be westering. The land was close now, so that he could see the rise of green hills and the jagged teeth of cliffs.

He had never been outside of Prydain, never sailed a ship on the sea. He craned to see this foreign country, this land of Lys.

It looked no more exotic than the riverbanks of his own country. The cliffs were higher than any river crags he had seen, but never as high or as splendid as the white cliffs of Dubris on the easternmost edge of Prydain.

The ship shifted under him. Something slid into the water just behind him, where a moment ago a sailor had been standing. He looked back down the length of the deck.

The crew were gone. He saw small dark shapes in the sea, darting away from the hull. Only his guardsmen remained, motionless and witless.

A wave caught hold of the ship and lifted it clear up to heaven. Goronwy wasted no time in terror. He wrapped his arms around the dragon's neck.

The sides of the ship rose up behind him. They looked like ribs, covering over swiftly with gleaming black scales. They swallowed the planks of the deck, the captain's station, the guardsmen standing unwary and unknowing where, but for a whim, Goronwy would have been.

The dragon's neck flexed within his grip, but he held on for grim death. What had been a ship was now a long, sinuous body and a serrated ridge of spines. Just behind him, a spiny mane unfurled.

Intentionally or no, it cradled him; it kept him from sliding backward, and held him in place as the dragon surged up out of the sea. Icy spray lashed his cheeks. Bitter cold surrounded him, but the fire of the dragon's body kept him warm.

He should have burned in that great belly. He clung for his life to the dragon's neck, as it flew over the crash and tumble of waves on the rocky shore.

It aimed arrow-straight for the black cliff with its veil of sea-ice. Goronwy's eyes clamped shut. He was going to die after all, flung headlong into solid rock.

The air changed. It was thicker, darker, and even colder. The dragon's warmth surrounded him like a mantle, or a spell of protection.

The great beast swam through earth and stone as a fish would swim through the sea. Goronwy tried to see where it was going, but his eyes found nothing but blind darkness. He squeezed them shut and buried his face in the warm scaled neck.

He was past fear. All he wanted to do was live. He held on tightly and prayed to any god or power that would hear, and tried to do nothing to remind the dragon of his presence.

The dragon undulated through the darkness. Time stretched into endlessness. Light dwindled to a dream, and then a myth, and then he had no memory of it at all. The whole world was the warm scaled thing he clung to and the roaring of his own blood in his ears.

STONE TURNED SUDDENLY to water, and darkness to a blaze of light. The air that Goronwy sucked into his lungs was living air, not water or stone.

The dragon lifted its head, swaying beneath a leaden sky. A deep lake glimmered below, with a small dark figure beside it.

For a moment Goronwy saw with the dragon's eyes: a morsel for its dinner, tiny and bony and hardly worth the trouble. Then with a small but potent shock, he recognized the master whose sorceries had brought him here— inadvertently as it might be.

The dragon stooped down until its head hovered eye to eye with the master. Goronwy's arms let go of their own accord; he crumpled in a heap on the shingle at the master's feet.

The dragon sighed as if relieved of a burden. He felt it subside behind him, sinking back down through the water into its native earth.

The lake seemed much larger without that great, breathing presence, and the air much colder. Goronwy looked up into Master Gamelin's face. There were words he could have said, but none came readily to his tongue.

If the master was dismayed that Goronwy had survived the journey, he betrayed no sign of it. He spoke calmly, even coldly, with no evidence of surprise. "Good morrow to you, sir. Have you brought it?"

Goronwy laid his hand on his purse where the tooth lay undisturbed by its long journey. He should have drawn it out for the master to see, but he made no move to do so. Out of shock, anger had grown. "Suppose I have. What will you do about it?"

That was frankly rude. The master's eyes did not even flicker. "You are resourceful," he said, "and stronger than you look. You may be more useful than I thought."

"Do you think so?" said Goronwy. "I would have thought you'd be happier with me dead."

"There is no room for weakness in the world that I would make," Gamelin said. "Now, sir. The key. If you please."

Goronwy's fingers tightened over the curve of it. "Maybe I should keep it, if it's so valuable. I've paid for it with my life."

"It is of no use to you," said Gamelin.

"Can I be sure of that? You tried to kill me for it. It must be worth a great deal."

"It is worth everything and nothing," Gamelin said.

"How mystical," said Goronwy. "What is it worth to you, then? What will you pay to have it in your hand?"

The master's eyes narrowed. Goronwy shuddered inside, not entirely with terror. That was power, this thing he had. He rather liked the taste of it.

Master Gamelin hissed, but he bowed to it. That was heady, too, and even more terrifying. "What price will you demand, messire?"

"I don't need gold," said Goronwy—he hoped that surprised the master. "Magic I've got, and you'll teach me as much as I'm able to learn. My price is simple for a mage as great as you. Give me what is mine. Give me Prydain—its throne, its people, all its magics. Give me those, and you may have your key."

"When the key has opened the door," said Gamelin, "you may have all that and more."

"But not now?"

"No," said Gamelin.

Part of Goronwy wanted to insist, to be strong and not give way. But he had enough sense to know that would be unreasonable. "Swear," he said. "Give me the great oath, the one that will devour you living if you break it."

No mage or sorcerer would take that oath lightly. Gamelin did not hesitate.

"I do swear," he said, "and if I break that oath, may the Great One itself devour my soul."

That was all Goronwy could have asked for. Still he hesitated. But he had made a bargain.

Slowly he drew out the Serpent's tooth. It gleamed in his hand like translucent glass. It did not look like anything that had come from a living creature, and yet there was perceptible power in it.

He was imagining, surely, that it was reluctant to leave him. The master's long thin fingers closed over it. A sigh escaped them both.

Once it was gone, Goronwy held his breath. Now, if ever, the master would dispose of him.

"Come," Gamelin said.

It was true, then: Goronwy was too useful to kill—at least for the moment. He had little choice but to do as he was told. The dragon was gone; there was only the lake and the wood that surrounded it, and a track that wound up from the shore into the trees.

Gamelin had already begun the ascent. Goronwy drew a deep breath. Nothing that he did here could compare with his long, wild ride through the earth on the neck of a dragon. Even if he died, he would have had that.

It was worth the price. He laughed suddenly, as if a great burden had fallen from him, and bounded in the master's wake.

23

THAT ESTEBAN HAD allies who were loyal to him rather than Gamelin, Averil had known since a year past, when she first came to the Golden Wood. She had met eight of them, and learned their names and faces.

Others now were scattered through the kingdom of Lys, taking souls and leading armies in the Serpent's name. Esteban expected to call on them when the time came. That would be soon: Averil's newly restored magic could feel the world spinning ever more swiftly toward the end of all she knew.

The Rose had died and been reborn, but that rebirth was perilously fragile. Lys was dying, losing souls with every day that passed. Now the blight had spread: she felt it in Prydain, where some great power had struck down the queen; she felt it in the kingdoms that surrounded Lys, in Gotha, in Moresca, in the remnants of Romagna.

She was supposed to have stopped all this. She should have come to the royal city, taken crown and throne, and put an end to all that her predecessor had done.

She would do that, but not as anyone had intended—on any side of this long war.

Now she followed Esteban out of the chapel into the hall, where another of his allies waited. This one, he had promised, would stand with them most strongly against the false priest, and bolster them in all ways.

Averil nearly turned on her heel and strode back the way she had come. Only a long habit of discipline—and the wall of guards across the door—prevented her.

Mathilde greeted Averil with a smile so warm she might almost have been taken in by it. Averil could manage nothing so warm in return.

It seemed her wintry greeting was sufficient. Mathilde came forward to take her hands, with a graceful curtsey. "Lady! I'm most glad to see you restored to yourself."

Averil had her doubts of that, but she bit her tongue and held her peace. "You have news," she said instead, as she slipped her hands free of Mathilde's.

Mathilde nodded. "Prydain's queen is ill, some say near to death. No one knows the cause, but she was found in the crypt of a church in Caermor, beside an apparently empty tomb."

Averil's hackles rose. "And? There's more, isn't there?"

"There may be," said Mathilde, and maybe she meant to be coy and maybe she did not. Averil had lost the capacity to judge her fairly. "Our late king's priest has been nowhere in evidence for the past handful of days, but before he vanished, he hinted that some great thing is coming."

Averil closed her eyes, but briefly: in the sudden darkness, she nearly fell off the edge of the world. "He's found it," she said. "It's in his hand. Lady, if you still have any friends on the Isle, you would be wise to tell them what you know—and beg them to send aid to Prydain."

"Prydain no longer matters," Esteban said, "if its great treasure has left it."

"Prydain's queen matters," said Averil grimly, "and she has powers that we can well use."

"Not now," said Esteban, "and not at this distance. It's all coming to a head, lady, and the center is here."

She damned him in her heart for speaking the truth. Every aid, every ally, every escape had slipped away. These two whom she did not trust were all she had left.

She had one thing, the great thing, the one they all were fighting for. If Gamelin had the Serpent's tooth, he would not wait long before he came to her. Then it would end— all of it, unless there was still, by some freak of fate, a way to stop him.

She could not see one. Granted, she had no gift for prescience, but she was trained in logic and in clear thinking. She had done everything she could to stop the whirlwind. It had only spun more strongly.

There was one last thing she could perhaps do. "Messire," she said. "Lady. Can you get me out of here?"

They stared at her as if she had taken leave of her senses. Mathilde said, "Lady, with all due respect, what good will that do? He'll only follow, and destroy whatever stands in his way. Here at least, no one is in danger but those of us who wish to be."

"That is so," Averil said, "and all logic says it must be so. But my heart tells me the solution is elsewhere."

"Where?" said Mathilde. "Not in Lutèce, surely, in the middle of a city, surrounded by innocents?"

"I'm not sure," Averil said. "But if that is where we have to go, we'll send the people away."

"Through the sorcerer's armies?" said Esteban. "They'll lose their souls before they've traveled a league."

Averil shook her head sharply, as if with that one gesture she could banish every glimmer of doubt or fear. "Just get me out; then I'll know where to go."

Prince and Lady exchanged glances. "Lady," said Mathilde, "we have allies and plans, and workings ready to set in train. But it's not time. We can't risk—"

"Everything is a risk," Averil said. "Are you with me or against me?"

Mathilde's answer was quick, easy, and apparently heartfelt: "Of course, lady!"

Esteban's was slower, but Averil found she trusted it more. "Tell us why we should go we know not where, to do we know not what, for what purpose even you perhaps do not know. If your only desire is to be free of this place, that will come to pass as soon as the priest comes hunting you with key in hand."

"I ask a great deal of you," she said. "Will you trust me?"

His dark brows drew together. After a while he said, "Lead. We follow."

"We'll need horses," she said, "and passage through the guards. And quickly. Time's flying."

She held her breath. This was the test: whether they would obey, and therefore accept her right to command them, or whether they would betray her to their erstwhile ally.

Esteban bowed, sardonic but obedient. Mathilde hid whatever objections she might have had behind the bright falsity of a smile. With Mathilde ahead and Esteban behind, warding Averil against the guards, they gathered what clothing and provisions they could, then made haste toward the stable.

There were horses as Averil had expected. Neither of these nobles was adept at grooming or saddling. Averil hissed at their ignorance, tightened straps and straightened saddlecloths and pushed them out the door into a world of ice and snow.

She nearly broke down weeping at that. The storm that had raged here rivaled the one she had sat out in Enid's house, and the cold that had set in after it was unrelenting. It was mad even to contemplate riding away from warmth and relative safety.

Her magic tugged within her like a needle to a lodestone. This was not the place where it needed to end. That other place was calling her more urgently with each moment that passed.

She kept enough sanity to wonder if this was another spell, bound to her magic. But if it was, she did not care. She wanted to end this. If this enchantment or compulsion helped her to do that, then she would give way to it.

She wrapped herself in her mantle and called in such warmth as earth and air had to offer—as much for the poor horse's sake as for her own. The snow was deep but soft; the sturdy brown gelding waded through it with surprising ease. She had no need for road or track. The magic showed her the way.

For all the weight of alien power that lay as thick as the snow on this place, Averil felt oddly light. A trickle of strength rose up out of the earth, a hint of wildness that in another time would have sent her flying back to the safety of more ordered magic.

Now she welcomed it. This was the power that lived in Gereint. Even so thoroughly sundered from him that she could not find him at all, this felt, somewhat, like coming home.

Amid the glow of renewed magic, she felt the darkness closing in, the bands of soulless soldiers roaming the Wood, and the army that clotted thick in the fields beyond, all the way to the shimmering mosaic of magics that was the royal city. There was no way out of the Wood but what the false priest allowed.

Averil would find a way. Esteban was faltering, losing the thread of the spell that protected them all. Mathilde's weaving was not quite strong enough to take its place.

One of them was going to break. When that happened, Averil knew where they would go. They wanted power. If they could not get it through their own machinations, they would turn back to the sorcerer who was so close to winning it all.

She fed them from the well of the earth's power. The shock of it nearly cast them out of the working, but she was ready for that. She basked for a moment in their astonishment and sudden awe, before she put it resolutely aside. There were hours yet of riding ahead of them, and the nearer they came to the Wood's edge, the harder that riding would be.

The track along which the magic led her was perfectly straight. Tracks of the wild magic always were—a bit of a paradox, since nothing else in that magic was either straight or ordered. As she followed it, she felt that the Wood that surrounded it was not always in the world she knew. That too was familiar, if not exactly comfortable.

Walls of confusion rose and fell beyond the track. Warring spells clapped together like thunder. The earth heaved; a great black shape rose out of it, swaying, giving off such a wave of heat that the snow turned to running rivers all about it.

Averil's heart stopped. The talisman rested safe above it, with the sleeper inside. This was no great serpent of the old world, although it was close kin: it was a dragon of the sea, a sea-drake, swimming in the dry land. She knew, deep in her bones where the magic was, that it had been compelled to perform an errand that gave it no pleasure. Now it turned, freed at last, toward the sea.

It was not the first such creature she had known, that had been so bound. Gereint had freed the other. There was no need for such a rescue here, but she offered the great beast a cool wash of power, a taste of its native element.

It bent down. Its eyes were as changeable as water, now blue, now green, now grey as rain. She had seen such eyes enchanted in glass in the perilous chapel of the Isle, and again in dreams and in glass within Lys: eyes that followed her, haunted her, shamed her with their grave and ancient wisdom. There was no evil, they tempted her to think. There was only fear, and misunderstanding as vast as all heaven.

The dragon's jaws opened. Something dropped from them into her hand. It was startlingly cool, round and smooth and gleaming: a dark pearl.

Averil's fingers closed around it. The dragon bowed, breathing the scent of hot metal around her, then dived into the earth.

Her horse shook from nose to tail, shocking her out of her trance, then snorted wetly and trotted onward. Averil tucked the dragon's gift into her purse. What it was for, she did not know, but she could not bring herself to cast it away.

She looked over her shoulder. The others seemed lost in a dream. Had they even seen the Serpent's kin, or marked what it gave her?

The gift was real. She assured herself of it, tracing the smooth roundness beneath the soft leather of the purse.

She lifted her chin and settled deeper in the saddle. The spell-weaving in the Wood was growing stronger. She had to save her strength, but neither Esteban nor Mathilde could hold much longer. She gave them as much as she dared, and prayed it would be enough.

The track went on through snow-laden trees, then descended into a shallow bowl of a valley. The trees were different here, lower and broader. Averil recognized the shape of apple trees, and pear, too. Beyond them was a stone ruin, which must have been the farmstead to which the orchard belonged.

That was not like anything else she had seen in the Wood, but it was hardly as strange as a sea-drake rising up out of the earth. There was fruit still on the trees, red and gold. Averil decided, somewhat abruptly if perhaps not wisely, to leave the track. The others needed to rest, and the ruins would offer shelter.

Tracks led into the orchard: prints of shod horses. Averil's skin tightened between her shoulderblades, but she had no inclination to turn and run. The earth held no foulness. The air threatened no danger.

Whatever was here, it meant no harm to her. She was not sure she dared trust that surety, but not enough to stop or retreat. The force that had been drawing her onward was stronger than ever.

It had grown to a kind of singing excitement, a promise of wonders. She pressed forward eagerly, on guard but without fear.

24

GEREINT WOKE FROM a dream of dragons and serpent's teeth and black pearls. He had not been asleep long: it was still daylight, and none of his companions had moved.

He rose and stretched. Mauritius took no notice: he was intent on the visions that danced in the fire. Lutèce was under siege, Prydain's queen lay near to death, and a man in black held up a thing that looked like a curved dagger of glass.

Gereint staggered as at a blow. Gamelin had the Serpent's tooth.

Did he know? Did he realize what Averil carried?

By the old dead gods, of course he did. How could he not? He had stymied them all at every step. The only wonder was that it had taken him so long to come to the end of things.

Gereint had never been prone to despair. He did not intend to begin now.

Maybe there was no hope of ever winning this war. It did not matter. He would fight until there was nothing left to fight for.

With that firm resolve to stiffen his spine, he wrapped his mantle more tightly around him and ventured out of the ruin. He moved with care, every sense alert. Magic was bubbling in the earth below: wild magic, magic untouched by any mage, human or otherwise.

He had a brief vision of a sea-drake swimming, improbably, in earth; then it vanished, and there was only blinding light and pure, blessed presence.

Some remote fragment observed that it could be a trap. He paid it no heed. She was here, riding out of the orchard, and to his dazzled eyes it seemed that the snow on the branches had transmuted into a cloud of fragrant blossom.

Not yet, he thought dimly, hardly knowing what he meant. He blinked hard. It was winter again, dimming toward evening, but Averil was still there, still riding toward him.

For a dizzy moment he saw through her eyes: the trampled snow, the ruin, the massive figure in front of it, wrapped in a dark mantle, motionless as a standing stone.

Then he was himself again—truly himself, as giddy as if he had drunk a vat of wine. She flooded into all his empty places, filling him like a tide of light.

It was the most natural thing in the world to step forward and hold her rein as she dismounted. It was utterly natural, too, if never proper, to take her hands and fill his eyes with her face, until there was no need to see it at all.

She made a sound half like a gasp, half like a curse, and pulled his head down and kissed him until his senses reeled. When she let him go, his mind was clearer than it had been since he could remember.

This was right. This was what should be.

In that clarity at last he saw who stood behind her. The woman he knew, and not with pleasure. The man he recognized, because Averil knew him.

She had her own shocks of recognition as Mauritius and Darienne came out of the ruin, with Ademar yawning and rubbing his eyes in the rear. There was a moment of perfect silence and keen-edged stares, and not friendly ones, either.

A great deal of magic was the shaping and ordering of symbols. The name became the thing, or an image of the thing begot the reality. Gereint felt it vividly in this place that time and the world's weathers had worn nearly to nothing: the Serpent-mages, the mages of Isle and Rose, and between them, Gereint and Averil, who were something else altogether.

As he recognized the pattern, he felt a deep and unexpected rightness. Shards of the world slid together, bound in a matrix of magic.

It was all one. There were no orders and no divisions. There was only magic.

No one else, even Averil, seemed to share that sense of unity, of order and balance. They bristled at one another.

Gereint was none too happy to see the traitor or the Morescan, either, but Averil's presence gave him such deep joy that it was difficult to make anything else matter.

He shook himself back into focus. The world was crumbling around them. However solid it might be here, elsewhere it was falling into ruin. They were here to save it if they could—if anyone could.

It seemed natural and inevitable to Gereint that out of

that rightness and solidity, Peredur should emerge, stepping from the air. Gereint could not say he was delighted to see the being who had sired him, but there was a kind of relief in it. They needed all the help they could find.

Not so for everyone there. The crackle of hostility sharpened; it stung Gereint's skin like a lash of sleet or gale-driven sand.

And yet, to his considerable surprise, none of it came from Averil. She looked at Peredur almost with resignation. He was more deeply a part of this than any of them. Of course he would be here, where they all gathered against the end of the world.

The Knight and the Novice and the Lady Darienne were openly glad to see him. The sting of hatred was nearly gone, nearly suppressed, but Gereint's eye leaped to the source: the traitor Lady with her lovely face and her black heart.

The sweep of Peredur's glance took in them all. He was as somber as Gereint had ever seen him. "Lutèce is fallen," he said. "The Knights have withdrawn to the cathedral with such allies as still remain."

"And yet you walk free," said Mathilde.

He did not dignify that with a response. It was Averil who said, "Let him be. We need him; he's here. My lord, messire, whatever you want to be called, do you bring any hope for us?"

"I came looking for it, lady," said Peredur. "All paths are closing or have closed. Such choices as we have had are fading fast. Lady, it's all in your hands now. The rest of us are only here to serve you."

If Averil had broken down and screamed or cried, Gereint would hardly have faulted her. He felt the impulse in her, but she conquered it. She squared her shoulders, swallowed audibly, and said, "Well then. Some of us have eaten and rested. The rest of us need whatever of both they can get. We'll see to that; then we'll face what we have to face."

Peredur bowed. The others lacked the will or the courage to argue. The two with her were out on their feet in any case, and their horses had no objection to an evening's graze in the field.

Averil was glad to stop, to fill her belly, to close her eyes for a while. She was gladder than that, by far, to do it with Gereint near her. He was no more capable than she of letting her out of his sight.

Neither of them cared any longer that the others could see. She saw Esteban watching them, saw how his eyes narrowed and his lips thinned. In the world of courts and politics and civilized discourse, she would have seen trouble there, and marked him for a jealous man.

Here, the stakes were too high for petty rivalries. Averil could hope Esteban was man enough to realize it. For the moment he held his peace, and held Mathilde in check, too.

Mathilde's antipathy toward Peredur was less explicable and more troubling. Peredur seemed oblivious to it. He sat by the fire, conversing softly with Mauritius—consoling him for the loss of the city and the danger that beset his brothers of the Rose.

No one was trying to console her. She drew up her knees tightly and rested her forehead on them and squeezed her eyes shut. A few tears escaped, but she ignored them. She was tired, she was scared, she was at her wits' end, and none of these great mages had any wisdom to offer. They had cast it all on her.

They were fools. Their folly had brought Lys to its knees, and none of them had the sense to stop trailing blindly after a hopeless cause, simply because her blood made her queen.

She sprang up abruptly. Six firelit faces stared at her. Somehow, in her few moments of reflection, night had fallen. She turned her back on the lot of them and escaped into the darkness.

One or two—Esteban notably—rose to follow, but Gereint flattened them with a barely audible word. She felt Esteban's shock, and the respect that he leavened with hearty loathing for the common lout who dared flaunt the blazon of the Rose.

In spite of herself, her lips twitched. Gereint was a great gawk of a boy, that was true, and a peasant into the bargain. It did not matter in the slightest.

He stayed close enough for protection but not so close as to crowd her. She crowded him herself, moving into his arms. They folded around her; his breath sighed in her ear.

He held her without either lust or urgency, though she could tell he paid a price for that. So did she; her body was a young thing, too. But she needed him there, just then, while she faced what they had both been coming to since this long dance began.

"Do you think," she asked him, "that I really am Melusine? That a soul can die and leave the body and come back again?"

"I don't know," he said, "but I'll wager my—Peredur does."

"Your father," she said, though he stiffened. "Yes, I know what you are. I don't think anyone else does."

"I don't know what anyone knows any more," Gereint said, sounding for once like the boy he was. "It doesn't change anything. I'm still bound to the Rose, and you'll still be queen, if there's any kingdom left to rule."

She nodded against his breast, and held him suddenly tight. His ribs creaked, but he offered no protest. Somewhat guiltily, she loosened her grip. "It doesn't matter, does it? Not really. We are what we are. We do what we have to."

He brushed her hair with a kiss. She blinked against a new spate of tears. The Serpent's prison burned between them.

He seemed not to feel it. She felt as if her skin were blistering, not with heat but with supernatural cold.

It was the hardest thing she had ever done to let him go, to step away, to say calmly, "I need a little solitude. Can you give me that? Just for a while?"

That did not please him at all. But he answered her prayer: he backed away. "Just for a moment," he said.

She held her breath as he hesitated, but after one last, long glance, he withdrew into the ruin. She heard the soft rumble of his voice, and Peredur's equally soft rumble in reply.

Neither of them would let her be for long. That was not so ill a thing: she had to move quickly before she lost her nerve.

She was not even sure that the working would succeed; she could but try.

It was time. She was whole; she was as strong as she would ever be. If she was fortunate, she would take the enemy by surprise.

She slipped the pendant from beneath her chemise. It felt oddly heavy on its chain, or maybe that was only her reluctance. She set her teeth and her will, and cupped the pretty, deadly thing in her hands and breathed on it.

There might have been words to say, but all she had was the opening of her will and her wards to the magic that was in her, the power she had fought all her life, that now was all the hope she had. *Come,* she said to the wild magic. *Come and take me.*

She held her breath. It might take a moment, it might take an hour. It might not happen at all.

Even prepared as she was, the rush of air took her aback. Her fingers closed convulsively around the Serpent's prison. The whirlwind swept her up.

Voices called behind her, edged with desperation. Something caught hold of her foot and held fast.

Gereint. She should have kicked him free. But she had spent all her strength of will on this summoning.

He let go, rising up through the tempest, riding it as he did everything that had to do with magic: as effortlessly as he breathed. Someday, she thought randomly, someone would find the limits of what he could do.

Maybe today. But for this moment, he had her in his arms again, and she did not thrust him away as she should in all wisdom have done. She gripped him as strongly as he gripped her—and with much the same degree of temper. However glad she was of him, she could have killed him.

The whirlwind howled around them. Wood and snow-clad field and ruin with its little speck of fire were gone. So were their allies, the mages whose help Averil had hoped for while there was still hope left.

She closed her eyes and disciplined herself to quiet. The storm of magic seemed to yield rather more willingly than her heart. The roaring faded. She drifted like a feather, soft and light, down to the solidity of earth.

25

AVERIL OPENED HER eyes. She expected to see the sorcerer in the cavern beneath the royal lodge, where the Serpent's image slept and the old magic was still strong. Instead she stood under night sky, heavy with cloud, moonless and starless. Bodies breathed around her. Stone walls rose beyond them.

No souls animated those bodies. They surrounded her, but they left open a path leading to a dark door. A lone torch flickered within.

She shivered. She had escaped this creature's captivity, found her magic and her heart, and summoned all the power that she was born to. Now she must venture his lair again, because she saw no other hope.

Gereint was with her. That changed everything. She unfolded her hands from the pendant so that it hung free and unconcealed, then squared her shoulders and strode forward.

THE PASSAGE WAS dim and torchlit. As she advanced to the end of it and ascended a stair, a conviction began to grow in her. It blossomed into certainty at the top of the stair.

She opened a new door on a passage that she remembered. It could have been any corridor in any castle or great house in any kingdom, but the number and shape of doors along it and the carving of beams in the ceiling above it could only belong to one place.

She had been brought to the palace in Lutèce, to the passage that led to the great hall.

Her steps slowed. This was a trap, neatly and mercilessly laid. She walked willingly into it, but there was no need to be more foolish than she could help.

She gathered such magic as she had—a whole singing tide of it, now that Gereint was at her back again. She steadied herself within and without. When she was as strong as she could be, she made her entrance into the hall.

SHE HAD BEEN careful to have no expectations. If there had been a nest of serpents and an army of soulless soldiers, she would have met them with equanimity.

There were soldiers, standing as guards. She saw no serpents, but there were courtiers enough—the full court, it seemed to be, in full and glittering array.

Some faces she recognized. Others looked to be of other kingdoms: dark and aquiline Morescan, tall fair Gothan, slight and wiry Romagnan. It was as great a gathering as she had seen under Clodovec, but something about it was lacking.

There was no laughter. There was music, but no one danced. Such conversation as there was, was muted; it died with the music as Averil stepped into the light.

These were as much prisoners as she. Whatever they

believed the world would become, they had no freedom here. The guards with their empty eyes barred every escape—a sight Averil knew too well. They had food, drink, entertainment if they wished it, but they were at the mercy of the one who stood on the dais.

He stood somewhat apart from the golden glitter of the throne, warded by guards even larger than Gereint. The way he stood was as eloquent as words. He needed no ornamented chair to rule wherever he pleased.

Averil knew him then, more thoroughly perhaps than he intended. He was old, older than gods, and if there was human blood in him, he had long since repudiated it. He had served the Serpent in its day; when it fell, he had lurked and crept through the shadows, gnawing his resentment, until he found a royal fool whom he could corrupt and make his own.

He had nothing but contempt for human creatures, and rankling hate that they should have ruled so long and been free of him and all he worshiped. Their magic had blocked and thwarted him for years out of count, until it buckled under the weight of its own complacency.

Revenge was a cold thing, serpent-cold. Yet he still needed humanity, if only to feed the great beast he hoped to raise.

He was a bitter and twisted thing. He had dropped the pretense of a human face; he regarded her with slitted yellow eyes set in a grey and hairless skull, his body narrow and unnaturally supple in its long black robe. The power that pulsed from him made Averil's skin burn and prickle.

Gereint moved as if to set himself between them. Averil

caught hold of his wrist. He froze. She willed him to be quiet, to have patience.

He was quiet at least. When Averil advanced down the length of the hall, he followed, looming large but saying no word.

The sorcerer took no notice of him. All of Gamelin's stunted soul was focused on the thing that Averil wore about her neck. She had half expected it to change its shape, to conceal itself in some new and unforeseen form, but it was the same as ever: a pretty trinket, bright with enamelwork.

She could have torn it off and flung it in Gamelin's face. The urge was almost irresistible.

She had a purpose here. If she hesitated, she would lose everything she gambled for.

She lifted her chin. In this hall full of lambs for the slaughter, she was queen. The sorcerer had the key, gleaming in his hand, but she held the power.

Without what she had, the key was useless. And he could not touch or command it. His every hope rested in her, mere mortal creature that she was.

She ascended the dais. He was barely breathing, his yellow gaze fixed on the pendant. His fingers clenched upon the Serpent's tooth.

She paused in front of the throne and turned to face the hall. A thought drifted past. That tooth was as long as her forearm. The mouth in which it had grown must be nigh as large as the dais on which she stood. The Serpent itself . . .

Both legend and scripture called it greater than dragons, mighty as mountains. This hall would barely contain a fraction of it.

Gamelin had to know that. He had served the Serpent. If he meant to free it here, to feed it and then set it free, then he must intend it to swallow the whole of the palace.

It would swallow all of Lutèce, and then all of Lys. It would swallow everything.

Not if Averil did what she had come to do.

She sat on the throne. A sigh ran through the hall. In a far corner, someone moved. Someone else spoke, a murmur of frivolity. A lute struck a note that led to another, that grew into a sprightly dance.

A lord approached a lady; his brother bowed to her companion. In a moment the hall was full of glittering, whirling figures, and a-shimmer with light and laughter.

There was a desperate edge to that laughter. Averil was both flattered and sad. Flattered that her presence should have roused them all so well; sad that they were all meant to die.

Gereint stood unmoving just below the dais. Though the hall was warm, he had not dropped his mantle. He was carefully not passing judgment.

Averil slipped softly into the parts of herself that belonged to him. He did not want to do as she asked. *I can't leave you again. Least of all to this.*

She held firm. They would not be parted in spirit again.

He was not so sure of that, but there was little he could do here, except be caught in the trap if she failed.

He slipped away through the swirl of bodies. It seemed he melted and flowed into the shadows between them.

Almost too late, Averil let the memory of him slip from

her mind. Gamelin watched her still, fixed like a snake on its prey.

He was waiting for something—a word, a moment. Averil did her best to give him neither. She sat as still as a painted image, while the court honored her and defied their captor by dancing the night away.

26

GORONWY WAS INVISIBLE again. Once he had given up the Serpent's tooth, he found himself relegated to the master's following. The master had no time for him. The end was coming at last, and all his mind and magic were focused on that.

When the young queen appeared, walking straight into the master's trap, Goronwy watched from among the court. No one saw him, least of all she.

He had seen her before. He had seen the hulking figure at her back, too—even more hulking than Dylan Fawr's young giant. They had both found him out in Prydain, when he did the master a favor: telling him what the queen and her allies did. They had called it spying and tried to make trouble for him, but his aunt had refused to believe them.

Queen Eiluned had been a fool, and well for Goronwy that she had. She was dead or near it now, and he was here, doing what he did best: spying.

He framed the thought without bitterness. When this was over, he would be a king, and if he spied, it would only be for his own amusement. In the meantime, he spied for his life, and for such power as he could gain.

When he saw this lady in Prydain, he had not looked closely. He had only seen the danger to his life and his secrets. Tonight in Lys, he had time to observe that she was beautiful.

It was not a courtly beauty. Her face was not painted, and her gown was unabashedly plain. She had obviously been riding in it. Her bright hair was drawn back in a simple plait; curls escaped from it, doing as they pleased.

He had never seen a woman who did not care whether she was beautiful or ugly. It was fascinating. It made him want her almost as much as he wanted to be king.

When he was king and she was queen, would it not be fitting that he should take her?

He hugged the thought to him, as his eyes ran over the hall, over and over—spying, as they did best. They came back at length to the man who had followed Averil to the dais. He hid behind a cloak, but Goronwy knew what was beneath. He belonged to the Rose.

When he turned suddenly and melted into the throng, Goronwy's nape prickled. A spy knew a spy.

This one was rather good at it, but not as good as Goronwy. He left just enough of a trail that Goronwy could follow it.

The Squire was sure of his invisibility: he aimed straight for his goal, with no doublings or diversions. He strode down the passage that led from the hall, then descended a stair.

No torches illuminated the passage to which the stair took him, but he shed his own light, a silver shimmer that danced ahead of him. There were shapes in it, inhuman and insubstantial. They were barely there; Goronwy would have thought he imagined them, if he had not known their like in Prydain.

That was not magic of the Rose. The young queen's loyal dog was brimming over with something older and stronger and wilder.

Goronwy's mind darted toward another big, fair, grey-eyed mage who was well known in Prydain. Was it possible . . . ?

Anything was possible, as Goronwy knew well. He strengthened his wards as carefully as he could without stopping or betraying himself. The Squire had the kind of stride that looked unhurried but stretched Goronwy's pace to a trot.

Goronwy hated these big, loping, arrogant men. He fed that hate into his magic. It rewarded him with knowledge: this was a deep way, a secret way, out of the palace and toward the prow of the Isle.

It opened in the crypt of the cathedral of the Mother. Kings lay buried here, and Knights, too, but no Paladins that Goronwy knew of. No Ladies, either, traitor or otherwise.

The Squire took no notice of the tombs that he passed. He ascended the spiral stair, two and three steps at once.

He nearly lost his shadow there. Goronwy's shorter legs were weak at the knees; his lungs were burning.

He had come too far to give up. He dragged himself up the stair as best he could.

THE CAVERNOUS SPACE of the cathedral had become an armed camp. In place of tents, there were curtains shielding the side chapels. Men gathered in companies down the length of the nave. Only the high altar remained solitary and sacred.

A webwork of magic held them all together. Parts of it were woven into the glass of window and lamp and reliquary. A little bound the stones of floor and walls and pillars. The greatest part dwelt in the minds and hearts of the men—not only Knights of the Rose but knights and lords of Lys and their loyal vassals.

There were more men here than Gereint had expected or dared to hope. Women, too, in the Ladies' Chapel, working the magic that held them all together.

Gereint found the Lord Protector Bernardin there, with the handful of Knights who were left alive in Lys, and a duke or two. They faced a circle of ladies whose faces Gereint too well remembered.

Darienne was not among them, and Peredur and Mauritius and Ademar were not with the Knights. Gereint paused at that; his heart clenched. He had expected that Peredur would bring them to this place, and the traitor Lady with them.

He could do what he had to do without them. They were safer in the Wood, please the good God, than they would be here.

He bowed to Bernardin and the rest of the Knights. The slant of a glance included the rest—even the ladies. The eldest of those seemed amused.

Bernardin wasted no time in courtly nonsense. "The others?" he asked.

"In the Wood," Gereint answered, "with the queen's mage from Prydain."

"But you are not," Bernardin said.

"I came to the city with the queen," said Gereint. "She's in the palace. She asks that you trust her, and that you do as she bids."

The Lord Protector's brows had risen. "What does our liege lady bid?"

"When the time comes," said Gereint, "you'll know. Rest well tonight, but be ready. At dawn it begins."

He heard the intake of breath around the circle, and felt the shudder of protest. But Bernardin bowed his head. "We shall be ready."

Averil needed no more than that. Her relief came to Gereint as a long sigh.

Gereint was not so easy in his mind. He could see the faces, and too few of them wore expressions that reassured him.

The eldest Lady caught his eye. She neither moved nor changed expression, but she let him see the strength in her. It was given, she made it clear, to the queen of Lys.

But would it be when she knew what Averil meant to do? Would any of them fight for her then?

Gereint had no choice but to trust that they would. He yearned desperately to go back to her, to keep her safe, but he had his orders, too. This night of all nights, he had to obey them.

His armor was ready—long before Gereint had expected it. The armorer had it waiting for him in the chapel of the Paladins. It fit well, with a little room to grow, just as Gereint had asked.

Magic was laid on it, as always on armor of the Rose, but

this was more powerful than most. Strong spells had wrought it, and strong spells protected him while he wore it.

They sharpened his senses, too. A niggle of unease had followed him from the palace. Now it mounted to an itch in the back of his skull. Gereint spun and sprang.

The shadow scratched and kicked and cursed. Gereint shook it to make it stop. He did not quite snap its neck.

It was a child—a boy, dark and wiry and small. On second glance, he was not as young as he had seemed. He was older than Ademar, a little younger than Gereint. Old enough to have a considerable store of magic and some skill in using it.

Gereint knew that face. It belonged in Prydain, sulking in the queen's wake. As to how it had got here . . .

The stink of Serpent magic was strong. So was the reek of treachery. If Queen Eiluned was dead, she was dead because of this—her own kin.

Squires and Novices of the Rose closed in. Gereint was tempted to leave the boy to them, but this was too slippery a snake to trust to anyone else. "I think," he said, "that you do not belong here. I'd be a fool to send you back to your master. You've done your best to kill your liege lady. Where in the world can anyone be safe from you?"

The boy could have answered—Gereint's grip on his throat was not particularly tight. He blinked, big-eyed, and shook so hard Gereint almost dropped him.

That was clever of him. Gereint bound the narrow wrists with a cord of magic and left him to stand or drop as he pleased.

He pleased to stay upright, swaying. His glance was pure venom.

"The smallest ones have the worst poison," said one of the Squires. He had been sharpening his sword; he let the light pour down the blade and drip like blood from the point.

Gereint shook his head, not without regret. "This is royal blood of Prydain, however sadly diluted. Best we send him where he can do no harm."

He had baffled them all, not least the boy from Prydain. It was probably not wise to do any of this, but time was short and Gereint was out of patience.

For all the weight of order on this place, for all the web of workings that was meant to choke the life out of anything either wild or serpentine, the earth beneath was pure untrammeled magic. Gereint had felt it in the cathedral square when first he came to Lutèce. It was stronger now, rising in response to the forces gathered above it.

Wildfolk could not come up through the stones of that paving. Gereint could send a mortal down into their waiting hands. Where they took him mattered little, if only they kept him alive and reasonably well, and saw to it that he did not escape.

Who knew? He might learn something. He might even grow into an honest man.

He was growing cocky as the silence stretched, thinking he saw weakness. That made it easier. Gereint lifted him with more than hands, and cast him into the earth.

27

DAWN BROKE WITH the clarity of ice. Averil watched the light grow from the window of a high chamber in the palace. It was a chamber reserved for guests; she would not sleep in either the king's chamber or the queen's, until she had won this battle.

She had been put to bed by servants who were not, to her surprise, soulless. They remembered her from her time in the palace before; their welcome seemed genuine. For their sake she pretended to sleep for a while, but she was too restless to keep up the pretense the whole night long.

There were no preparations to make, except to try not to think about what she would do when morning came. She found the library that shared this tower with the guest chambers, and from its bounty chose a book of old poems frivolous enough to divert her for a while. But in the deeps of the night, even that palled. She curled up in a window embrasure well padded with cushions, and waited for the night to pass.

GEREINT FELT THE sun's coming in his bones. Everyone he could see was up, eating or drinking if he could bear to.

Those who wished it heard mass at the high altar, sung by a venerable Knight who brought beauty and power to the familiar rite, and bound together the souls of those who celebrated it. The working ran like a tide through the cathedral; it touched every man and woman within those walls. It flowed over Gereint like cool fire, melded with the magics in his armor and made itself a part of his shield.

Other workings took shape among the Knights and the Ladies. Every mage who had the art or the skill was raising power and shaping it into either a weapon or a defense.

Gereint's working would come when it was time. He was not a praying man; he was not sure he would call himself a servant of the good God or his son. Nonetheless he knelt for a while before the altar of the Paladins.

It was quiet there. The few men who were still in the chapel were absorbed in their own prayers or preparations. The only sound was the soft chink of metal as a grizzled Knight finished arming himself with the help of a very young Squire.

Strange to think of this as the chapel of his kin. Twelve tall windows completed the half-circle of the chapel; the farthest on the right was Peredur's. He stood there as a young man, a boy, in silvered armor, with his fair hair shining in the light of a rising sun. Instead of a sword he carried the Young God's war banner, a long streamer like a trail of flame.

Gereint had no banner to raise, unless it was his magic. He turned from his father's window to the first of them, far on the left. There was Longinus, lord and commander.

Often he was shown as a man of some age, bearded and

going grey, but here he was young. He was tall and broad and strong; he raised his spear against the powers of heaven, but two small children played about his feet.

Gereint swayed dizzily. For an instant he had felt the haft of the Spear in his hands, and heard the clamor of battle, and known in his heart the sorrow that he must take to his grave for the lover whom he had lost.

Whether that was magic or memory, Gereint had no time for it now. Companies had begun to draw up ranks in the nave. Gereint had his own to go to, under Bernardin. He schooled his mind to silence and his magic to stillness.

He rose just before the singing began. The Ladies in their chapel had begun a sacred chant. Their voices echoed in the vaulting, sweet and eerie.

As he came to his feet, deep voices rolled forth from the high altar. The Knights had raised a response.

How long had it been since the Rose and the Isle performed a working together? Surely not in living memory.

He paused a moment to drink in the wonder of it, before he buckled on his sword and slung his shield behind him.

THE SERVANTS BROUGHT a frugal breakfast of bread sopped in wine. While Averil choked it down, they laid out the full splendor of court dress, and stood by to bathe her and dress her in it.

The bath she took. The gown and the jewels she would not. Her riding clothes were clean at least, and mended where they needed to be.

The only jewel she would wear was the one she wished she had never heard of. It hung heavy and burning cold on her breast; she could feel it even through the wool and linen of gown and chemise.

When she was as ready as she could be, she did not wait for Gamelin's blank-eyed slaves to come and fetch her. She went out alone to face him.

She passed the pair of blank-eyed soldiers who had barred the door through the night. They stood like images carved in stone.

They did not follow her—and that, she had not expected. She went on with head up and shoulders back. All her defenses were armed and ready.

So early still, with the sun barely up, the palace was unwontedly quiet. She began to wonder if the court had managed to escape, or if, God forbid, the sorcerer had taken more souls to feed his power. She had sensed nothing of it in the night, but she had been hoarding her own strength, bracing for the morning.

She strode down the empty corridors. She had meant to seek the hall, but as she drew near it, she found she had no desire to go in. The sorcerer had taken his stand in another place.

He had left a track for her to follow. There was no chase now, no desire to escape, and they both knew it.

The palace gate was open. The guards stood with legs braced and spears upright and eyes fixed forward. Again, as Averil passed, none of them moved.

As soon as she had left the gate behind, it boomed shut. The sound shook her to the bone.

She could run away still through the silent city under the grey and lowering sky. She could leave it all behind, death and doom and damnation, and save herself—for a while. If she cast away the Serpent's prison, that while might be rather long.

She could not do that. She was not bred for it. She was made to be a fool, whether holy or unholy, blessed or damned. At the moment she was not sure which of those she was.

She raised her eyes to the towers that rose beyond the palace. The Mother's cathedral stood serene, belying the tumult that both filled and surrounded it.

The sorcerer's army lined the square before it and the streets that led to it—all of them, every one, save only that which led from the palace. Rank upon rank barred the gates of the cathedral, barricaded it with bodies and with edged steel.

But the square itself was empty. One lone figure waited in the center.

There was nothing vulnerable about him. Power cloaked him. The staff on which he leaned was a great weapon of sorcery, and a terrible memory. It was the Spear of Longinus, wound with the Young God's Shroud. Now it belonged to the Young God's enemy, twisted to his purpose. Serpents twined up and down it, perpetually in motion.

He had no doubt that Averil would come to him. When she could see the serpents clearly on the Spear, she paused. The wall of armed men had closed behind her.

She was perfectly calm. Just so, she thought, must Melusine have felt when she faced the same terrible choice. She had not gone as far as Averil meant to go, but through her, her allies had saved the world.

There was no Young God here, no Ladies, no Paladins. Only Averil and the ancient creature who had seen his great master fall.

Averil was past wondering whether she had made the worst choice of all; the one Melusine and her companions had not been able to make. As Gamelin drew forth the Serpent's tooth, drawing strength from Spear and Shroud, she cupped the pendant in her hands.

It was burning cold. She set her teeth against the pain of it.

Sometimes she had fancied she felt the creature sleeping inside, dreaming its long dream. That dream was ending. The tooth that had come from the Serpent's own body called to it as like to like: one of the oldest and simplest of all magics. The Young God's blood fed it. The power of Spear and Shroud joined together with it.

The clouds had begun to swirl overhead, slowly at first and barely perceptibly. As power rose in the earth beneath her feet, the motion above grew swifter.

Winter's cold battled the sun. Earth and sky made war on one another. Within the cathedral, a trumpet rang.

The great bronze gates burst open. Light blazed from a hundred jeweled windows. Shards of it pierced armor and flesh, cleaving the sorcerer's men asunder.

The black army closed in upon the Knights and their allies. Dark blades rose and fell. Bright blades clashed with them, but few, so terribly few.

Gamelin smiled. These were no gods or Paladins. They were mortal men, mages to be sure, but they had no power to stop what had begun. Their desperation doomed them.

Averil let his contempt slither past her. The more of his slaves died, the less strength he had. But there were so many.

She wrenched herself back into focus. Gamelin had raised the Serpent's tooth.

The pendant twisted in her hands. Almost too late, she tightened her grip within and without.

The sorcerer's lips moved. The words he spoke were in no human language, a pattern of hissing syllables. The tongue that shaped them flicked between sharp-curved teeth, long and thin and sharply forked.

The spell was strong. It muddled Averil's wits and stole her will.

She sank roots in the earth. Magic surged up in her. It was wild magic, forbidden magic, the magic she had been taught never to touch.

It was the only magic she could trust. All the rest was lost or broken or destroyed. She thrust down the last of her fears, opened wide and embraced the wild magic.

The walls of the Serpent's prison cracked. The sorcerer's chant rose to fill the world.

He expected her to fight: he built his spells on it. They fed on her resistance.

She dropped all of it, let it fall. As he floundered, over-whelmed by his own strength, she seized the reins of the spell.

For an eternal instant, she had the power to stop it, to wrench it aside. She need not do what she had resolved to do.

The instant vanished. She flung the whole of herself into

the spell. She was edged like a weapon, keen as a sword. If all gods and the whole of heaven allowed, that sword would destroy a power more ancient than gods.

She reached for the power of Spear and Shroud. Even corrupted as they were, they knew her. Her blood called to them. They bent to her will.

The walls crumbled and fell. The ancient working shattered. The Serpent woke.

28

THE WORLD HELD its breath. Earth and sky hung poised. Even the wild magic stood still.

The Knights and their allies held a few precious and hard-won yards in front of the cathedral. They stood on the bodies of soulless men, now lifeless as well.

Somehow Gereint had found himself in the lead. People kept following him, maybe because he was big enough to bull his way through.

Certainly it was not for awe of his skill with a sword. He could hack his way through a line, which was a considerable improvement over his earlier prowess, but he was glad to have his brothers at his back.

When the spell broke, he was nigh as incredulous as the rest. It seemed to have occurred to none of them that Averil would be the one to do it. They were braced for Gamelin's victory, not for what seemed to be her betrayal.

Gereint had been braced for it. But when it happened, he realized that he had not believed it. Not in his heart.

She had her reasons. Most of them were mad and the

rest were simply desperate. But truly, he had to concede, there was no other choice.

He raised his shield and his voice. The sound that came out of him astonished him as much as it did the rest. It throbbed in the earth; it rang in the air, deep as drums and clear as the call of a trumpet.

It caught hold of the web of mind and spirit that bound the brothers of the Rose. It encompassed all of their magic, their arts and skills, their souls and their bodies.

Shield locked on shield. Magic locked on magic. One man, one mage, could never stand against this power that rose. An army of them joined together, bound under a single will . . . that was a different thing.

The sorcerer had seen the power in that. But he had taken souls from bodies, and so broken any will they might have had. The binding of the Rose was never so tractable, but man for man, it was stronger. Much, much stronger.

More than the Rose was woven into it. The Ladies had come out behind the Knights, armed and armored as they were. Where the shields of the Rose were black adorned with a silver rose, theirs were shining silver without mark or device.

They locked together with the shields of the Rose. They brought with them the power of the Isle: all of it, drawn from the deep wells of earth and sea and sky.

Yet a third power bound itself to them. He had come out of air like a spirit of fire: bright armor, bright shield, last of the Paladins. Two Ladies followed him. A Knight and a Novice slid smoothly into the line where they belonged.

Peredur took his stand beside Gereint. There were still

matters to settle between them—that went without saying. But Gereint greeted him with soul-deep gladness.

His golden shield locked with Gereint's black-and-silver one. His power lay open for Gereint to take or leave, use or discard, as he pleased.

"As *you* please," Gereint said, "Father."

Peredur bowed his head. "I please to do as you will, son and brother. Long ago I followed you; now I do so again. My will is your will. Command me; I obey."

"Stay with me, then," said Gereint. "Fight beside me. Pray, if there's any god you pray to."

"There is one," said Peredur.

His eyes lifted. He did not mean the one who rose up out of the earth—Gereint did not think so, even for a moment. But Gereint could well see why one might worship such a creature.

It was more like a dragon after all than a mortal serpent: a great cold-drake, greatest of them all. It was beautiful— for all Gereint had heard and known and seen, he had not expected that. Its scales glistened in the chill grey light, red and gold, blue and green. Its eye was as broad as the rose window of the Mother's cathedral, deep gold, ineffably ancient and subtle and wise.

Its head swayed above the cathedral's towers. Much of its body still coiled in the earth. Its forked tongue flicked, tasting living air for the first time in twice a thousand years.

A swirling cloud of wildfolk danced above it. More of them came as Gereint stared, streaming from all the quarters of the sky.

They were drawn like moths to a flame. So was all magic

that was in the world, of whatever shape or kind it might be. Gereint felt the tug of it in himself.

A gnat buzzed down low, stinging the Serpent with darts of magic. Amid the small sharp pains, it offered relief for the Serpent's hunger and its long thirst.

He was clever, that sorcerer. He put Gereint in mind of a snake-tamer at a fair, undertaking to subdue the creature with a mingling of pleasure and pain.

He was strong. He drew strength from a multitude of souls, and from long years of magic nurtured and hoarded against this moment. He cast a net over the Serpent, and tightened the coils, bending it to his will.

Averil's high fierce cry struck Gereint like a dash of icy water in the face. All the power she had gathered, all the magic that was in the well of the world, blazed in her hand like a sword of fire. She raised it to sever the Serpent's head from its body and destroy it forever.

And she hesitated. She looked into those vast golden eyes and saw, not ancient evil, not the devouring of souls, nor even the scourge of all that lived and walked upon the earth. She saw a living creature in torment.

That torment was the danger, not the creature itself. The sorcerer's working gnawed at the roots of things. It unmade all magic but its own. It fed on immortal souls.

The Serpent's hunger was a simpler thing. It needed meat, as any creature did. It yearned toward the armies that swarmed in the square.

The sorcerer lashed it back without measure or mercy. It hissed in pain.

Gereint was a child of his age after all: he shrank from

the thoughts that filled his head, heresy so terrible it damned him even to frame the thought. How strange that Averil, who could barely abide either the wild magic or the daimon Peredur, could look on the Serpent and see no evil.

She had learned to accept wild magic. Surely Gereint could learn to see the Serpent as she saw it.

Once more she called the wild magic to her. She drew on Gereint's strength, which was the strength of the earth itself. With the full force of it, she smote not the Serpent but the sorcerer.

He barely felt the sting. His armies made him too strong.

Gereint roused his own army, as small as it was. Bless every man and woman of them, they shook free of shock and horror and came readily to his hand.

They charged the ranks of the sorcerer's slaves. The shieldwall mowed them down.

"LADY!"

Averil started nearly out of the working. Prince Esteban had appeared from the old gods knew where. He gleamed in his black armor and his crimson cloak: lovely and deadly, and smiling as if he had no care in the world.

"Lady," he said, "you cannot do this alone."

"I am not alone," she said. She could spare no power to brush him off, and that was a pity.

He stretched out his hand. Before she could shake him off, he had woven his fingers with hers. "Let me help you, lady. Let me be your consort—truly, in mind and magic. We'll master the Great One together."

He was strong, she granted him that. He had spells that

rivaled Gamelin's. Even as she paused, he sent one coiling around her working, feeding it not only strength but knowledge.

The Serpent swayed. Gamelin's working faltered.

Esteban struck past the Serpent and the sorcerer's working to the sorcerer himself, like a dart of fire. The sorcerer's wards drank it in, feeding on it. Gamelin laughed, a harsh and mirthless sound.

Esteban smiled. He poured magic upon those defenses, inundated them, drowned them.

Just as they collapsed, Averil smote the sorcerer. Esteban's blast of power struck hard upon hers. She followed it with another and another and another—caring nothing for the cost.

The swarm of wildfolk fell upon Gamelin, buzzing like maddened bees. He flicked them all aside.

In his distraction, he had left the working to itself. The Serpent shook free. Before Gamelin could move, before he could find his focus again, the great head darted downward.

Gamelin knew an instant's incredulity before those gleaming teeth, so like the one he still held in his hand, snapped shut where he had been.

The Serpent reared up. Its long throat pulsed as it swallowed its first meat in two thousand years.

It swallowed the sorcerer's magic with his body—and with it the spells that both Averil and Esteban had cast against him, and strongest of all, its ancient bane, the Spear that had subdued it so long ago. After twice a thousand years, that was little enough, but it flowed through the Serpent, filling it with new strength.

The Serpent swelled and stretched and grew, towering above the cathedral. As it grew, so did its hunger. It needed meat, indeed—and magic.

It snapped at the swarms of wildfolk. Most were quick enough to escape. A few followed the sorcerer into the Serpent's belly.

Averil drew up magic from the well below. As she did that, she wove wards, walling it off from the Serpent, so that it could not devour the magic as soon as she raised it.

The Serpent swayed within the bonds that Gamelin had laid on it, that Averil's working had strengthened and secured. Its eyes were on the armies that fought around the edges of the square. Its tongue flicked; it hissed. Its anger was rising. It was hungry. It must eat.

Wait, she willed it.

It did not want to wait. It needed to feed.

Soon, said Averil.

The whole of her mind fixed on that silent struggle, her will against the will of a force greater than gods. It fed on gods. Gods and magic were its dearest sustenance.

The Young God's Paladins had not left the Serpent alive out of mercy. They had had no power to kill it. Even if they had . . .

Averil was close to knowledge so vast and so potent that it beggared understanding. But the mortals around her were oblivious.

None of the sorcerer's slaves had lost either will or strength. Lesser sorcerers led them, allies and servants whose only hope lay in winning this battle.

They had the advantage of numbers. There were hundreds, thousands of soulless soldiers, and the good God knew how many commanders, each bound to carry out the master's plan. Averil felt the force of the geas in the air she breathed, a stench like cold death and hot iron.

The shieldwall of the Knights pressed onward. Where it passed, the soulless died. But there were ever more of them, and they knew no pain or fear. They rained arrows on the moving fortress. Now and then, however strong the wall, a bolt pierced it; a man fell, dead or sorely wounded.

Averil had no weapon but the Serpent. But if she unleashed it, it would feed on men and magic, and grow ever larger, ever stronger. She could barely hold it now. Once it had swallowed the enemy's armies, no power, mortal or immortal, could hope to master it.

"Lady," said Esteban, drawing her to him, wrapping arms around her, "bind your magic with mine. Quickly."

Averil lowered her eyes from the sky, where that monstrous head dipped and swayed. Esteban's smile for once was quenched. He wanted the power, of course; always. But he was honestly desperate.

"Let her go."

Averil had felt Gereint coming, leaving the shieldwall behind. In her heart he streamed flame, like a comet cleaving the night sky.

Her eyes saw a warrior of the Rose in silver armor, armed with a sword and a rioting fire of magic. His deep blue cloak billowed behind him as he ran, light in that weight of steel.

Esteban flung up walls against him. He passed them as if they had never been there at all.

Even at the end of things, Averil spared a moment's amusement at Esteban's shock. No one ever expected that particular gift.

Gereint halted in front of them. His sword's point hovered a hand's width from the prince's throat. "Let her go," he said again.

"I think not," said Esteban.

Averil hissed at them both and twisted, but Esteban's grip was too strong. She moved in closer, as if in surrender. He tightened his embrace as she had hoped he would.

She turned in his arms, seeming to soften, to give herself up to his greater strength. Her knee snapped up.

It met his steel-gauntleted hand. He spun her outward. If he thought to hold her then with a dagger to her throat, she was happy to disappoint him. She twisted free.

He barely noticed. Nor did Gereint. They bristled at one another.

"You, sir," said Esteban, "are a disgrace to your order. Your very presence dishonors her. Did you even dare to dream that your peasant blood could mingle with blood of Paladins?"

"He is not—" Averil began, but they were past hearing any voice but their own.

"She doesn't want you," said Gereint. By accident or design, his accent was more broadly rustic than ever. "She'll never give in to you."

"Among grubbers in the earth," Esteban said, "that may

be true. We children of Paladins are more practical. Defiance is the resort of the powerless. We know better than to argue with destiny. And she," said the prince from Moresca, "is destined to marry among her own kind."

"Destiny is no longer what it was," Gereint said, slanting a glance at the creature that loomed over them all.

"So," said Esteban. "Would you do battle for her?"

Averil could have slapped him. And Gereint—the idiot, the blazing fool; he tipped up his chin and said, "Unto the ends of the earth."

The Serpent hissed. It had caught the taste of her anger. For an instant it nearly slipped free.

With both of her too-devoted allies lost to all sense or reason, she had no one to help her sustain the working. She could not even speak; any word, any distraction, and the great beast would overwhelm her.

If they survived this, Averil would throttle the pair of them. They never even noticed. Already they were circling. Their dance of death had begun.

29

AVERIL'S ANGER SEARED Gereint's bones. He had more than enough doubts of his own, but he also had a plan. It was not much of one, and it rather grandly ignored his lack of skill with the sword.

The heart of it was a thing he had seen, that he was quite certain she had not. The Serpent had destroyed the sorcerer, and that was a great good thing. But the power that ruled the armies hid itself behind a handsome face and courtly manners.

He was a good liar, that mage from Moresca. If Gereint had not had the gift of seeing through any mask, he might have believed the man when he declared that he had come over to Averil's side.

He was on no side but his own. He fancied Averil as a man fancies a fine mare, for her beauty and her lineage and the glory she could bring him.

He did not intend to share her with anyone, whether friend or lover, ally or servant. She would rule the Serpent, and he would rule her.

It was a cunning plan. A courtier might even call it elegant. Gereint the farmer's son had a much more earthy word for it.

He raised his voice until it boomed across the square. "Single combat, then, messire. You and I, blade to blade, to the death. Winner takes all: war and victory, lady and Serpent. Will you swear the oath with me?"

He held his breath. He had wagered everything on the man's blood and breeding: that he would be unable by his nature to refuse such a challenge.

Prince Esteban stabbed straight to the heart of the flaw in Gereint's logic. "What, I should fight a duel of honor with a commoner? Should I so degrade myself?"

Gereint sucked in a breath. "I am a Squire of the Rose, messire. Only sons of Paladins may enter that order. Who was your ancestor, then? Was it Santiago the Blessed? Did he not take to wife a village witch?"

Prince Esteban drew himself up. He was as tall as Gereint, though never as broad. "My father is a king, and my mother a queen. Whose by-blow are you, then? Surely not Clodovec's."

Gereint raised his sword. "Surely not," he said. "Come, messire. Or are you afraid you'll lose?"

"You wield that blade like a mattock," said Esteban.

"So then," said Gereint. "Teach me to wield it properly."

That, at last, even this strong mage and clever conspirator could not resist. He sprang upon Gereint in a whirl of flashing steel, so swift and sudden that Gereint fell back in dismay.

The diversion had succeeded: all around the square, the

sorcerer's slaves faltered. But it had to last, and Gereint was grossly overmatched. He had the strength to withstand the rain of blows, but not the speed or the skill to match them.

Without armor he would have been cut to ribbons. With it, he felt the strain of blow after blow after blow. His shield took the brunt of it, but the prince's blade darted persistently toward his head, nicking and denting his helmet, until his ears rang and his vision swam.

He had given up even trying to strike back. All he could hope for was to buy time for the men of the Rose and the mages who fought with them to bring down the enemy's army. He hardly needed to feign weakness, to fall back step by step, away from the looming shape of the Serpent.

A presence slipped beneath his awareness, growing slowly lest he be distracted to his death. It filled his body, poured down through his legs and arms. His retreat slowed; his bladework quickened. The art that had been so difficult revealed itself for a thing of beauty and bone-deep logic.

He felt a brush of warmth that reminded him of Peredur's smile. Any outrage that might have struck him at such an invasion, he kept for later. It was saving his life now, and with it his foolish cobble of a plan.

The Morescan began to give ground. His speed was no less, but Gereint's had grown to match it, with greater strength in back of it. He drove the Morescan back and back, as coolly merciless as the power inside him. His arm never weakened, never tired. Every stroke the other struck, he was ready for it, turning it, battering his enemy as his enemy had battered him.

The shieldwall of the Rose had cut down a swath of soulless soldiers. Arrows swarmed upon it. From within the wall, a bolt of power leaped upward. The arrows fell in a rain of ash.

But there were more and ever more of the enemy. They seemed to rise up out of the ground, pouring in from all sides. The shieldwall stopped perforce, beset wherever it could turn. The mages within struck and struck again, but their power was not infinite.

Now. The thought was Gereint's, and Peredur's, and even Averil's. Gereint called up one last surge of strength and skill, beat aside a renewed attack, and struck the Morescan down.

Gereint stood swaying over the body. Peredur's presence withdrew as softly as it had come. The point of his sword sank to the paving; blood stained it, bright and dreadfully beautiful.

He had killed with magic before—a great slaughter of king's men, which was a mortal sin, and he would pay for it in his time. But he had never taken a life with edged steel, hand to hand, eye to eye.

As the life ebbed from those clever dark eyes, the waves of soulless soldiers slowed. One by one at first, then in companies, they lost their will to move, or else wandered aimlessly.

Too many still fought. Lesser mages led them, but they had lost their unity of will. The one great attack had broken into skirmishes. Company turned on company—by accident or design.

They seemed to have forgotten the Serpent, even as they

clashed beneath its shadow. Averil's will and power held it still, but its hunger had grown immeasurably.

Gereint let fall his sword. The duel had taken him halfway across the square. The broad space had been empty then; now knots of men skirmished all around and through it.

Gereint darted around a knot of men locked in combat. None of them ventured near Averil or the Serpent. She had raised wards so potent that the soulless who stumbled into them fell dead, but he passed through unhindered.

She reached for him with hunger to rival the Serpent's. Where she stood, the well of magic was deepest. He gasped with the power of it. It surged up through his body and into Averil.

It was pure magic, wild magic, unsullied by any rule or order, and yet every order was contained in it. Gereint opened eyes that saw the whole tapestry of the world with all its magics.

That was the Serpent's vision and its knowledge, and its greatest hunger. Its nature was to be a devourer of worlds.

Or was it? Need it be? It was born of magic, steeped in it. Both gods and mortals in their time had endeavored to rule it. But it was not of its nature evil. Like magic itself, it was whatever its wielders willed it to be.

What if, Gereint thought; or maybe Averil, or maybe both. What if . . .

The Serpent had rooted itself in the well of magic. If they destroyed it, if that was possible at all, this world's magic would die. If they let it be, or if they freed it, it would feed and feed until it was sated. They could imprison it again; mages of the Isle and the Rose pressed for that, as the only choice that they could see.

They were as blind as ever. Gereint framed the thought without contempt.

He looked down into Averil's eyes. He saw the sky reflected in them, and the wildfolk that filled it in uncounted multitudes. They were airy creatures, hardly more substantial than the clouds they had displaced, but in their way they were wise. They went where the magic was, and all of it was here.

They had no fear of the Serpent, though it tried to feed on them. Some even leaped down its maw, laughing as if dissolution were the greatest jest in the world.

It stooped abruptly and swept up a long swath of the warring armies. They died in silence, without a struggle; almost as if in relief.

Averil's shock brought the massive head about. It was growing even as it moved, as broad now as the square, and its body swelled, driving Gereint back. He dragged her with him; she went unresisting, fixed once more on the Serpent.

"Set it free," Gereint said.

She rounded on him. "Are you mad?"

"Just do it," he said. "Listen to your heart. This thing should never have been bound at all, by any will or power."

Her head shook. "We can't. We'll destroy everything."

"We won't," Gereint said.

She opened her mouth, but no words came. Her hands were cold in his. Of all the things she had done on this terrible day, this was the hardest.

"I'll do it, then," he said.

As he gathered his power, she stopped him. "Both of us," she said. "It has to be both."

He nodded. She was shaking, but her mind was made up.

She had always had the knowledge and the trained skill. Gereint had the strength, all the way down to the heart of the earth.

He gave her all of it. She reeled, but he was there to steady her. The Serpent swayed above them. Its anger was rising.

He was the sword, she the hand that wielded it. She was the mind, and he was the heart. They were one power, one spirit. One body.

Gereint had lived in Averil's body and she in his for long enough that there was no shock in the passage from one to the other. They knew well each other's differences: how they walked, how they balanced, where their garments bound and where they hung loosely, and what parts of them were most tender to the touch.

And yet they had schooled themselves strictly in their days together. They might touch, they might kiss, but they went no further. They must not.

Truly they believed they had succeeded; they could live in the same house, ride in the same company, labor side by side, and seldom even think of what their bodies wanted. It was both discipline and sacrifice. They were as proud of it as any holy anchorites.

In the Serpent's shadow, as their power swelled, their vaunted discipline shrank into folly. If they denied this, they weakened their magic immeasurably.

This was the core of their power. This that they had, this thing that they were, was as old as the world. It was the Mother's first creation and Her most beloved.

He was in armor and she was dressed for bitter winter. They stood in the middle of a battle.

None of it mattered. She drew something from between them, round and darkly shimmering: the dragon's gift of gratitude for her compassion, the black pearl. It grew as the Serpent had, until it swallowed them, and swallowed the Serpent, and became the well at the heart of the world.

The square was gone, the armies, the cathedral—all gone. They stood on the Serpent's coils, an undulating pavement of jeweled scales. The sky was a dark pearl; all magic was contained in it.

Gereint's armor had vanished with the mortal world. So had every woven or hand-wrought thing that belonged to either of them.

Averil swayed toward him as he swayed toward her. His heart was hammering, but no more strongly than hers.

The Serpent breathed above them. It was caught in the spell as they were. Its hunger, its fury, had grown strangely remote.

Warmth enveloped them all. It began at the root of Gereint's spine and surged upward and outward, magic so strong, so pure, it swept his soul clean.

It was all one. Gereint, Averil, the Serpent, the manifold worlds and all that dwelt in them—so many faces, so many forms, but the heart of them all was the same.

Averil's body fit perfectly into his. Her mind and magic

flowed through his own, until there was no telling where one of them ended and the other began.

The Serpent's breathing slowed. Its anger dissipated. Its hunger melted into theirs, and as they were sated, so was the Serpent. The light of it, the jeweled brightness, shimmered about them. Some of it was edged and shaped and contained like glass; some was pure light, free of the world, flowing into all that was.

Gereint opened his eyes to find them full of Averil's face. Red and gold of her hair, green and subtle blue of her eyes—she had taken that great power into herself, and therefore into him. Yet it was all around them, in the air they breathed, in the light that shone on them: enormous and ancient and wise.

The Serpent had swallowed the world, and the world was whole—all one at last, and free, and all its magic made anew.

30

THE SUN STOOD as close to the zenith as it could come in the dark of the year. Its warmth bathed the faces of worn and battle-wearied Knights and Ladies, lords and men-at-arms and common folk who had emerged from hiding.

Men in black armor wandered in confusion. Their eyes were alive; their minds were their own, and their souls were in their bodies. They had no memory of the war or of their part in it.

All of them, whoever and whatever they were, stared about them in wonder. Wildfolk were everywhere, dancing in the sky, walking on the earth, perching on roof and tower. The air was full of shadows and sudden lights, of wings and eyes, of voices that laughed and sang.

Gereint had his armor again, but it was no longer silver. It shimmered with scales of red and green, blue and gold. The rose on his shield had turned to gold; a jeweled serpent coiled about the stem.

He rather envied Averil. She was no more or less beauti-ful than ever, and no more or less magical. The pendant still hung between her breasts; it was empty now, but somehow it had kept both its power and its mystery.

He had given it to her in love and longing. It kept the memory of that. When he touched it, his finger stung, even through the gauntlet.

He pulled off both gauntlets, and his helmet, too. Just as he began to wonder if he had dreamed the pearl and the magic and the rest of it, Averil met his stare.

He wheezed as if he had been struck in the gut. She flushed just visibly, but then she smiled. Deliberately, in front of all the world, she kissed him long and deep and sweet.

THERE WERE MIRACLES enough, but the world was still for the most part itself. The kingdom of Lys had a great deal of healing to do. The orders and the Church crept forth as the good citizens of Lutèce had done, blinking and bewildered, but determined already to have their way in this new world.

The wild magic appalled them, but it was no longer the fragile and retiring thing that it had been for so long. It was everywhere, in everything, and it meant to stay.

Averil had a world's worth of work to do. If she stopped to think about it, she would lose all her courage; therefore she determined not to stop.

She had feared that the Rose and the Isle would turn against her for what she had done, but when she faced the Knights and the Ladies at the battle's end, they all bowed to her, every one, even the pale and much subdued Mathilde.

They bowed to Gereint, too, to his lasting confusion, and to Peredur, until he bade them stop. But they would not. They knew him now, had seen what he was in the midst of the battle.

Neither of those two could go back to his old obscurity. Averil forbore to pity them—or to spare them, either. She needed all the strength she could get, and the last of the Paladins and his mightily magical son had more than enough for her purposes.

"YOU ARE A hard, cold, cruel woman," Gereint said to her.

He was not angry with her. If anything, he spoke with admiration. She allowed herself to be glad of that.

It had been a handful of days since the Serpent swallowed the world and made it new. Tomorrow Averil would take the crown in the Mother's cathedral—a hasty coronation, some said, but necessary. She needed that circlet of gold and the powers both mortal and magical that came with it, to heal this sorely wounded kingdom.

Tonight, for once, she had a moment to herself. Gereint had been trying to efface himself among his brothers of the Rose, but she had summoned him to the palace. Slightly to her surprise, he had come.

He could have refused. She had laid no compulsion on him. As it was, he came late and somewhat ruffled from a swirl of duties and obligations that rivaled her own.

It was always going to be like that. She was queen, after all, and he would be a Knight soon enough.

But one thing had changed with the change in the world. "I've spoken with your commanders," she said, "and with certain personages who are entrusted with the keeping of the laws. One of those laws is about to be changed. I may be a cold, hard thing, but, messire, I need you now and always. We'll not be sundered again."

"We won't be, lady," he said. "Not in the spirit."

"Nor in the body, either," she said, "except as need and duty require. When I stand before my kingdom tomorrow, messire, you will stand beside me. I'll take my crown and my consort together, and begin as I mean to go on."

She had expected some response—she had hoped for joy and braced for a sputter of protest. He was silent for so long that in spite of herself she began to be afraid. When she looked into his face, it was as blandly opaque as his father's.

At length he spoke, and not to set her heart at ease. "You're not asking, are you, lady? Is this a command?"

"Does it need to be?"

He spread his hands. "You are my lady and my queen."

"You won't lose anything," said Averil. "The Rose will change, because it must. The court . . ." She shook her head. "Well, there's no denying who your father is; you're the image of him. If you're a few dozen generations nearer the source than the rest of us, then that only makes you stronger. They'll decide you're all the rage."

"Some of them already have," he said grimly.

"It's not so bad," she said. "There's so much to do and undo, we'll hardly be in court at all. Mostly we'll be—"

He stopped her babbling with a finger on her lips. His face was his own again, and his eyes were as warm as they had ever been. "Lady," he said, "truly, I don't mind them. They need something useful to do, most of them, but we can give them that."

She heard that *we*, as he had intended. Her heart swelled. She veiled it in temper. "You knew!"

He nodded with no sign of contrition. "Mauritius called me in before you did. He wanted to give me a choice."

"Since he didn't think I would?"

"Since he didn't think I could refuse you, no matter how much freedom you left me."

"Did he want you to?"

Gereint lifted a shoulder in a shrug. "He said he wouldn't turn you away, if he were in my place, but I had to decide for myself."

"And have you decided?"

He looked full on her then, seeing all of her that there was to see, in all ways and worlds. No one else could do that, nor ever would.

He never did say the words. It did not matter. There would be words enough tomorrow and in all the days after, and deeds enough, too, for both of them, side by side, one heart and one spirit, though they might not always be of one mind.

That made her laugh even through the kiss. He drew back, neither surprised nor affronted; but he did love to look at her.

She would have to learn not to blush when he did that. Still, she had her revenge: he blushed even more furiously than she did, and spluttered wonderfully when she called him beautiful.

"I am not—"

"You are," she said, "and I am hard and cold and merciless, and we have a world to mend."

"Both of us," he said with a touch of wonder.

"Both of us," she agreed, "now and always, as we always have been."